Cipher Sisters
c. 2013 ThunderDome Press
ISBN: 978-0615854236

Typesetting and design by Michael Paul Gonzalez
Cover Design & Photography by Michael Paul Gonzalez

Interior Photography by Aleks Bienkowska

Additional Photography

Amanda Gowin: Page 77 collage, first and last pages,
You and Me title photo, *Mercy* title photo

Michael Paul Gonzalez: Page 104

Vintage photos from the collection of Aleks Bienkowska

This book will be released in electronic format, but its primary goal in design is to remind the reader of the simple pleasure of holding the printed work in hand. It's small enough to take with you to spread the word far and wide: the paper book is not dead.
Show it. Share it. Help it survive!

CIPHER
SISTERS

edited by
Amanda Gowin & Michael Paul Gonzalez

THUNDERDOME
PRESS

Deciphering the Sisters

There's something magical and a little spooky in the idea of twins - a shared womb, a mirror that answers, the ideal best friend granted by the universe. There's little mystery for me as to why this perfect Other would be enough, in the way of companion, confidante and co-conspirator. Not having a twin leaves us alone in the world to search and fumble for all of these things, ideally in one person eventually we'll call our mate or love or spouse, someone to spend the rest of our lives with, making our brains compatible. But to be born with the other half of yourself? As children we all pretended to have a twin at one time or another, didn't we? Imaginary friends, pets, playmates - maybe they were all stand-ins for what we hoped our twin would be: someone who knew the insides of our brain. When I first read about the real Miller twins, I ached for the loss of such perfect symmetry in the world. For over seventy years, the two of them had (in my imagination) what we all want from any human interaction. Enough. And everything. Their story was beautiful in its lack of detail. What use had they for any of us? Here, we are eighteen outsiders, peering into a crystal ball that divides and rejoins endlessly. We are poking at a puddle of mercury.

- Amanda Gowin, editor

An abandoned house is a paradox, lived in, yet vacated. Furniture, clothing, photos, all of it evidence of life, maybe vibrant, maybe stagnant, now frozen in amber. Forensically, you can look at artifacts, and you can make assumptions about the people who were there, their personalities, dispositions, dreams, failures. You can ask around for people who knew them, get second hand accounts, but you'll still only be tracing an outline of the person who lived there. Our Lucy and Darcy are fictional, but still we're at the crossroads, listening to those who knew the sisters, those who claimed to know them. Twins, two separate bodies but joined from birth all the way to death. They leave behind evidence of a long life, fully lived. In their wake is mystery. Echoes of echoes that will only continue to distort through time. Given enough time, everyone's life will become that abandoned house. Will people know you by the guideposts you leave? How long will those markers stand? How long until you become a ghost?

-Michael Paul Gonzalez, editor

TABLE OF CONTENTS

Dance, Darling by Richard Thomas 1

A Witch in West Kansas by W.P. Johnson 5

The Cipher Sisters in: Saga Sideshow by Tone Baker 20

Mickey Slim by Chris Deal 33

You and Me by Adam Autin 36

That's Showbiz by Jason Matthews 39

Mercy by Rebecca L. Brown 45

1971 by Ken Goudey 47

Regular Earharts by Andrew McElrath 52

There's No Business Like ▮▮▮▮▮ by Xander Stronach 56

**The Chance Meeting at the Backstage
of the Apollo Theatre, Harlem NYC** by Sek Han Foo 58

Real Lookers by Audrey Hare 64

**The Cipher Sisters and Kid Nosferatu
Dance the Bally-Kootch** by Edward Morris 68

Asymmetry by Amanda Gowin 74

Darcy and Lucy Among the Flowers by Alexander Davis 78

Lucky by DB Cox 83

1951 by Matt McGee 89

The Sister is The Sister by edward j rathke 98

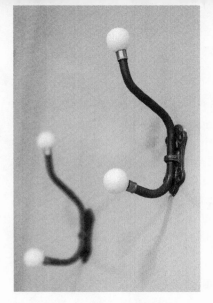

Dance, Darling
Richard Thomas

To see them in the grocery store, with their hair all pinned up, their faded grey suits freshly pressed and their red lipstick blazing, they were somebody's grandmothers, eyes twinkling, hushed conversations over grapefruit and green onions, their secrets buried deep. But if you looked close, there were hints of something more—faded ink on both of their wrists, concurrent numbers of 140603 and 140604. If you watched them fill up their grocery cart, you'd have to look close, for the bottle of cheap bourbon nestled in between heads of lettuce and bags of hard candy. The prescription bottles were quickly shuttled into their leather purses, a quick smile to the pharmacist, no eye contact between them, the nightmares that would come later that night still hours away. They wouldn't talk about it in the daylight, Lucy with her blonde wig hiding the radiation treatments, the cancer long gone, but the shadows and screams still right around the corner. They talked about very few things that mattered, in the daylight, Darcy chain-smoking, her dry skin like faded parchment, her bloodshot eyes always rimmed with tears, pushing the cart across the linoleum, one wheel rattling out of sync.

The boys would help them to the car, sunshine on them like a searchlight, a moment in each of their tiny bird hearts where their ribcages rattled, wings fluttered, and the echo of gunshots caused them to stutter a step, grab the young man by the bicep, and gasp in hushed voices—curses muttered to the hot tar of the parking lot below their clumsy feet. They apologized, always, but the boys didn't mind. The sisters were part of the history of the store, always together, never just one. They tipped $1 and only $1, whether it was a grocery cart overflowing with toilet paper and family size bottles of aspirin, or a bag of apples, fresh from the local orchards. Nobody knew if their last name was actually Cipher, because they always paid in cash, never with a credit card, never revealing that little bit of history. And when Lucy and Darcy pulled out of the parking lot in the long Cadillac, something out of the 1970s, a car that Johnny Cash might drive, black death stretched out forever, their wraparound sunglasses comical on their withering faces, the boys would wave, and pause for a moment. For under the floral perfume was a hint of something sour, something going bad.

It wasn't much of a choice, the dancing, the games they had played, the roles they fulfilled. They told each other, over rocks glasses splashed with amber liquid, ashtray overflowing, the sun setting behind torn blinds and faded drapes—that they had no choice at all. They were children then, five years old—too young for labor, worthless in the eyes of the pale demons that descended on the captives with random acts of violence and hatred. The gas chambers were always there, a threat that was never empty, faces they knew constantly disappearing, their parents long gone, the screams of their mother like talons over their cold, white skin, slicing them open—the dead eyes of their father two dark orbs that would float in the night sky for eternity. They shut down, Lucy and Darcy, the tears that flowed only drawing more attention, the rough hands of the guards eager to shake them, to bark orders at those that stood around them. "Stille," they would yell, "Stille das kinder." Silence the children. So they went mute.

Years. A lifetime expired. And yet, they survived, the sisters. Not without effort. Darcy in a bathtub, the razor long and eager to nip, her forearm opened up as a sacrifice, the numbers carved out and left floating on the surface of the crimson water. Lucy learned first that they were inseparable, now—always within earshot, always a head cocked listening for the silence that meant success had been found, death recognized with a loving embrace. No, not on her watch, she'd mutter. And when she finally could hold Darcy up no longer, sinking into her own darkness, a needle and a spoon, again it was her arm that begged to be broken, severed, stabbing at the fading ink that branded her skin, numbers that reminded her of what she was—a commodity, a piece of meat, something to be sorted, stacked and put on a train to a distant land. As if hearing a noise that only a twin can hear, Darcy appeared in the doorway, out of breath, her waitress apron still on, her fast hand slapping bare skin, Lucy trembling and crying out in anguish, the open hand coming again and again, across her face, knocking her to the floor, snapping the syringe in half, holding her as they collapsed to the floor.

The men knew they were damaged, but they filled the room anyway, lined the stage, as the Cipher Sisters danced. It made no sense, the dancing. It triggered hazy memories of phonographs spinning, glasses clinking, men in dark uniforms, fires blazing in stone hearths, women in pearls laughing the death laugh of survival, hands on shoulders, lips at ears, hems rising up in an effort to coerce. "Tanzen, lieblings," the women would say, settling in whatever lap was free, the men like wolves with their teeth bared, hair bristling beneath their caps, skulls trembling with dark deeds. Always together, the rooms lined with mirrors, the stages ringed with dull bulbs, holding each other up, pushing each other down, as the dirty money fell to the stage floor, wadded up, folded in half, tucked in garters and gathered with shaking arms. They were lost. Backstage they would find each other again, pick up the pieces, filling their handbags with rent money, whispers and cigarette smoke, empty pint bottles dropped into garbage cans. "Dance, darlings," Darcy would chuckle, "If only for a moment."

They filled a library with black and brown leather journals, wall to wall and floor to ceiling. They put it all down, in excruciating detail, never sharing, never reading, just channeling the darkness, vomiting out the suffering, in an effort to rid themselves of the poison that had seeped into their bones. On a good day they would smile at each other over grapefruits and green onions, knowing they were broken, knowing that it was futile, but unable to surrender, not now. They would place bent hands with swollen knuckles on the shoulders of the boys and the world would not crush them. And then, on the way home—the long, black car slicing the sunshine, prowling the back streets, a predatory grin in polished chrome, their only defense against the shadows that followed them—they would stop at the railroad tracks as the gates fell down, as the lights flashed and the whistle blew, hand shooting out to grasp for each other, smiles pasted on their faces, ignoring the cattle cars that flew by, the faces staring out, the screams never ending, and they would cry quietly in the black car, and say nothing—not a word.

Fractured, worn out, the library full, the refrigerator empty, stomachs tied in knots, they would lie down on the king sized bed they shared, and close their eyes. The papers would say they died within weeks of each other, but that was a lie. As if sharing the same breath, Lucy and Darcy listened to the phonograph that looped over and over, and they held each other, apologies whispered, until the could hold each other no longer. They let each other go, hands at their sides, wrists scarred with pink mottled tissue, their efforts in vain, ciphers no more.

A Witch in West Kansas
W.P. Johnson

Ned drove east towards the rising sun, stopping when he reached the end of his property. The sun was a squinting eye over the prairie, setting the fields of wheat on fire as the stalks swayed in the soft wind, hunched over and nearly ready for harvest. He parked his truck on a road that divided his land from his neighbors, a No Trespassing sign slightly bent before the field.

Standing between the two wheat fields, Ned made a couple of tight fists, feeling the dry scratch of his calluses. He walked up to his own crop and dragged his hands through the drooping stalks. A cool wetness coated his skin. Tiny droplets of condensation had yet to rise off the wheat, leaving the prairie a fiery sky of stars blinking under the rising sun.

He walked back to his truck and sat inside with the door open. He waited. It would take at least another hour or two before the field was dry enough to test.

He prayed. He wasn't very religious, not in the way some men felt that all things in life should be laid at the foot of the cross. Ned felt that a lot of things in his life were left to his own hands. Who would mend the fence around their property or build a fire when it got cold? In the end it was up to him to take care of business and provide for his family.

Him and his wife Cynthia had named their daughter Eve, a name from the bible. Maybe he wasn't religious but he didn't mind a little insurance in case God was paying attention.

Eve hardly spoke these days, especially now that it was nearly harvest time again. The scars had finally faded to a pink groove that bridged

5

across the arteries on her wrist. When it was stitched together with horse hair, Ned could hardly stand the sight of the black Xs. Then the scabs fell off, revealing a pale line of new skin. He took notice of how well she had healed, thinking she'd be healthy again come spring time. It made him sick to think of the scars in those terms, thinking of Eve like she was just another thing that he was harvesting.

Maybe not, Ned thought. Maybe this year the woman won't want an offering.

A small cluster of clouds loomed to the north, inching towards him. Bringing rain, or maybe hail. The sight of it was timed perfectly with his thought that things would be different this year, making him feel a fool. Of course the woman would get her due just as she always did and no one would do anything to stop her or refuse payment. Still, every time there was a storm Ned couldn't help but fantasize about a tornado ripping through the woman's house. Then when it was time to pay her, they'd find her feet poking out from under a tree, and all the families would get together and sing ding dong the witch is dead...

Ned shuddered to the term 'witch'. It was supposed to be something you'd only find in a movie or a book. It wasn't the kind of thing one was supposed to come across in west Kansas. Yet here he was, staring at clouds in the horizon and feeling like it wasn't up to God if his crop was ruined or not.

After a few hours passed, he stepped out of his truck and walked over to the field of wheat, running his hand through it. It was dry enough to test. He glanced over his shoulder at his neighbor Harris's field. A thin sheet of clouds sponged up the sunlight and the prairie grew dim. Curious, he crossed the dirt road and walked into the opposite field, ignoring the bent trespassing sign. He grabbed a handful of wheat and separated the chaff from the grain, tossing several bits into his mouth and chewing. It gave a satisfying crack.

He groaned. Part of him wished that Harris would've held out. It was the same way you'd wish someone else would tell the boss to go to hell and quit a job you hated doing yourself. Yet no one ever did. People just groaned and carried on working, hating every second of it.

He turned around, letting the stalks of wheat brush his bare arms as he crossed back onto the dirt road. He took slow steps towards his own crop, as if another minute would make a difference as the sun picked off the remaining drops of dew. Crossing the threshold, the wheat gently clawed at him, leaving his skin dry. He grabbed a handful of grain, crumbling it in his hands and shaking away the chaff.

He placed the grain in his mouth and chewed.

It was soft and wet. It was as he knew it would be.

"Damn it all the hell," he said. He got back into his truck and drove home.

§

Cynthia prepared a lunch of turkey sandwiches with wilted lettuce and soggy tomato. She wasn't sure why. No one was very hungry, especially her daughter Eve, who spent all day in her room. Cynthia didn't mind and left her alone, doing all the chores herself. Every still moment made her anxious, making time a thing that crept towards her instead of passing her by, like a slow moving tornado.

Cleaning the knife and setting out the bucket helped distract her despite everything. A pile of dry wood had already been stacked in the fireplace. Clean linens sat in a basket along with some string to tie a tourniquet.

She brewed a pot of coffee, another unexplained act. She wasn't tired, despite having not gotten any sleep. All night long she lay still, thinking. Perhaps Ned had done the same and neither slept without the other knowing, thinking of their daughter, bone white after having nearly bled to death.

When the sound of a truck gnawed the dirt road, she dumped the first pot and brewed a second, wanting it fresh for her husband. He came in through the door, saying nothing. A soft bale of wind brought dust in after his businesslike footsteps. He stopped by the kitchen table and looked at the food that had been laid out. There were three sandwiches cut in triangle halves and a small pile of chips in the middle.

Cynthia pressed a hand to his arm.

"So?"

"It's like it always is. Our wheat is still wet. The wheat on Harris's property is bone dry, which means he already paid her." He looked at her hand. "Where's Eve?"

Cynthia rolled her eyes, expressing a vague kind of guilt. "Up in her room." She took a step back. "She's been in there all morning."

Ned nodded. White hairs of steam came off the pot of coffee. He poured himself a cup and blew the heat off before sipping. He eyed the sandwiches that had been laid out on the table, feeling sick to the idea of eating. A long breath came and went from his lips and he grabbed one of the triangles, squeezing it into a ball. Thin drops of tomato juice bled from his hand. He shoved it into his mouth and barely chewed before swallowing. It hit his empty stomach like a rock and he sat down at the kitchen table, squirming to the pain in his gut. When it finally faded, he sat up straight.

"We'll do it tonight," he said. "Get it over with so it's not over our heads."

"She's been losing weight... she hasn't eaten anything today. I think she knows," she said. Ned furrowed his brow at her and she blushed to her own statement. She sat down across from him. "What I meant to say was... I know that she knows. But it's like her body knows too and won't let her eat nothing."

"I know. We'll have to make her eat something and get her strength up. She gave us a real scare last year when she passed out."

"You probably bled her too much," she said, locking eyes with the pile of chips.

Ned glared. "You know I don't take any more than what the woman asks for."

"Then she's asking for too much."

"Well what would you have me do?"

"I don't know," she shouted back. "Tell her it's too much and offer less." Ned said nothing and she added, "Have you talked to her about another offering? Like a pig, or money, or—"

"Damn it Cynthia," he shouted, smacking the table. The coffee mug and saucer rattled against one another. "You talk about this like we've got a choice or something. Do you think I enjoy watching Eve bleed like that?" He lifted the coffee pot, set it down, lifted his water glass and found it empty. When his hands ran out of things to do he spoke in calmer tones.

"She's my daughter too but you act like it's nothing to me, like I talk about it the same as slaughtering a pig. Well it's not like that. No matter how many times I do it, it doesn't get any easier."

Several tears fell from Cynthia. She swatted at them, mashing her middle finger under each eye and rubbing them dry. "I don't know," she said. "I guess I just keep hoping there'll be something else we can do."

"It's not fair," Ned admitted. "I know it's not fair. Honestly if I thought we could just get up and leave, I'd pack up the truck right now and hit the road. But we both know we got too much tied up in this stretch of land to leave it all behind." He stood up and came behind her, setting a hand on her shoulder. She shrugged it off at first, then leaned back, letting it settle.

"We just gotta make due," he said.

"It's our little girl..."

"I know."

"She's getting smaller and smaller... like she's disappearing or something."

Ned took his hand away, looking at the table with all the food he wouldn't eat. All the food Eve wouldn't eat.

"If she isn't sick or nothing, we'll fix her up something good, her favorite food. And I'll take care of bleeding her tonight." He watched Cynthia for a response. The woman's shoulders twitched as she lifted her hand and grabbed one of the sandwiches. She took a small bite and held it in her mouth, chewing. She swallowed the hunk of food the same way she'd swallow a mouth full of sick.

Ned turned away and left her, climbing the stairs. When he reached

Eve's room, he leaned in and pressed his ear against the door. He wasn't sure what he was listening for. It was cool to the touch despite the dry heat. The only sound was a low groan one heard when pressing their ear to anything. He gave a single knock and let himself in.

Eve lay on the bed under a pile of blankets. Her cheeks and neck were thin, sunken in. The faint light of her room only made the depth of her sunken face darker.

"Hey there sweetheart."

"Hey daddy." She remained laying on her side, staring out the window. Several strands of blonde hair branched out over the husks of her eyes.

"How are you feeling?"

"Good."

He walked up and sat beside her, laying a hand on the layers of blanket that hid the sharp cut of ribs. "You know that it's nearly time for harvest?"

"Yes," she said, staring out the window.

"I need you to eat something." He rubbed her shoulder. She felt cold and hard. "Whatever you want to eat, mommy will make it."

"I'm not hungry."

He held onto his smile despite it's want to leave him. "You passed out last time. We don't want that to happen again."

"I didn't pass out," she responded. "I died."

The air in the room went still. Ned froze, not wanting to disrupt it.

"What?" he whispered.

"I was dead," she said. Her eyes turned in their deep sockets and found him. Her voice was a steady wind that barely cooled the sweat off his brow. "I was watching myself bleed to death. Mommy was in the kitchen, cleaning. Wasn't any need for it, but she was cleaning, like she just wanted something to do."

"Eve," he said, grabbing her hand, the pale bump a wristlet over her vein. He could feel her heart beat. Her skin was cold. She returned her gaze to the window.

"You want to know what it feels like?"

Ned turned away, looking out at the window. It held a clipped view of their property. The flat expanse of the prairie faded away near the horizon until the beginnings of sky started. A single cloud in the distance was the only moving life within the view of the window. Even in the daytime there was something haunting about the great expanse of the wheat fields. At night, Ned could only imagine how the field must play tricks on one's mind, how Eve probably closed the curtain as to not turn to it and find such things staring back at her while waking from a dream.

"Being dead… it feels like nothing."

"Eve…"

"But it's weird, you know? Cause how could it feel like nothing if," she said, stumbling on her words. "I don't know how to say it. Cause nothing isn't anything, right? But that's how it felt. Just years and years of nothing, and no feeling or sound or anything at all. Like a big empty field in the middle of the night, and no matter how long I run through it, there's more field and there aren't any stars to see where I'm going. And I'm just… feeling myself disappear."

Ned closed his eyes and squeezed his daughter's bony hand. "I'm sorry Eve."

"Yeah," she said. "I'm sorry daddy, but I'm just not very hungry. All that nothing I felt left a giant knot in my stomach."

Ned got up from the bed and walked towards the door. When he turned to look at his daughter, the dimness of her room made her look less like a little girl and more like the skeleton of a dog that was drying out and shrinking, letting the wind eat away at it piece by piece.

"I'll be down in a minute daddy," she said, staring at the prairie.

"No," he said, shaking his head. "You just stay in bed. Don't worry about doing nothing for now."

"Really?"

"Yeah, let's not and just say we did."

"Okay." She wiggled under the layers of blankets and sat up. "What about…" She grinned and blushed two bruises over her cheeks. "You said mommy would make my favorite food. Whatever I wanted."

"Well, I did make a promise of that. You're right." Ned gave a gentle laugh. "What'll it be sweetheart?"

"I want ribs. Pork ribs… and corn bread," she said, thinking of more. "And corn on the cob, and sweet lemonade, and watermelon, and coleslaw, and… a pickle."

"Ha, is that all?"

"And chocolate cake," she added. "Yeah, a big piece of chocolate cake."

"Your wish is my command," he said, winking. He closed the door and went downstairs. When he reached the last stair his face held the ashen shade of a dusty cloud. Cynthia remained at the kitchen table. Ned walked past her to one of the kitchen cabinets and took out a bottle of whiskey and a single glass. He poured himself a generous drink.

"Is she gonna eat?"

Ned swallowed the whiskey. It burned going down but he didn't show. Nothing seemed to show on him. "Yeah. She'll eat."

"Good," she said, fidgeting with the table cloth.

"Gonna have to slaughter a pig. She wants ribs."

"Ha… well she really is hungry then isn't she?"

"Yeah." He poured another drink of whiskey. After, he went into the living room where the fireplace was, finding the bucket alongside the towels and the knife. He lifted he knife, checking the sharpness of the blade. There was a small section that was chipped with rust. He decided he'd sharpen it really good before using it.

He walked through the kitchen and out the back door with the knife and the bucket. Cynthia called out to him.

"You'll clean that before using it on Eve, won't you? Don't want her getting some kind of infection."

"Yeah," he said, "cross my heart and hope to die."

He went out with the knife and the bucket and found the largest pig.

§

The woman's house was nearly an hour drive west, several small towns removed from Dodge City. It was a small house surrounded by worthless land where trees never seemed to grow and flowers never bloomed. Life was strangled by a constant dim sky that hovered above her and the only thing she seemed to grow in her garden were beds of rock.

He parked his truck. He had reached the house around dinner time with the blood. Gray clouds lay like used up steel wool left out on a worn table, the sun having been buried underneath all the dirt and grime that had been kicked up from the earth. The house was small with a single window. A chimney spun out black cotton, stitching itself to the steel wool in the sky.

He stepped out of the truck and walked around to the passenger side, carefully lifting the bucket. During the trip it had shifted and the blood had sloshed out onto the floor of his car. It was nearly three quarters full, more than what he usually brought her. Some of it had congealed. He found a stick by one of the dead trees and stirred the blood the same way he'd mix a can of paint.

He felt the outside of the bucket. It was still warm to the touch from the fresh blood. Rumor was a family three farms away from Ned lost a crop one year cause they let the blood get cold before getting it to the woman. Or they had given the woman horse blood. There were a lot of rumors. Ned couldn't help but shut his mind out to all the stories he heard as he walked up to the front door and gave three knocks.

This time it don't matter what I'm giving her, he thought.

The door opened seconds later.

"Co?"

Ned wanted to look away, just set the bucket down and leave. Instead he gave the woman a long stare. He had never looked at her much before, preferring to forget that she existed as soon as their interaction was over.

She had a bent nose with a single wart that looked like an overfed tick struggling to stay latched on. Her lips were dry and pouty, falling over a mouth of crooked teeth. Her eyes were nearly black, the pupils perpetually dilated, the eyelids always half closed and worn looking. Bone white skin was marked by early signs of age and a fresh set of crow's feet. Her slender neck disappeared under an unwashed black cloak. Strange, but Ned had never thought her beautiful, yet there was a strange allure to her the longer he stared.

"Co?" she said again.

Ned presented the bucket. The woman grinned, rubbing her hands together. She gripped the bucket from both sides and looked deep into the freshly spilled blood.

"Dobry," she said to the blood. She looked up to Ned and arched her eyebrows at him. "Jestem glodny." She nodded and walked back into the house, setting the bucket next to a small fireplace. Already there was a small pot cooking a stew of carrots and potatoes. Even from a distance Ned could see that the stew was black.

"Czernina," she said, noticing that Ned was looking at the soup. She rubbed her stomach and gave a satisfying moan. Ned took a step inside. The woman frowned and stepped back.

"Is that soup?" he asked, trying to sound friendly. He pointed at the pot. "Soup," he said again. "Is that soup?"

The woman fidgeted to his presence. "Czerina," she said again, nodding. "Soup."

"It smells good." He rubbed his stomach. It was a soup of blood and root vegetables, smelling of the earth and death. It was impossible to not feel the smell of it filling his lungs like a mouth full of a coffin dust.

He pointed again. "Could I have some?"

The woman frowned. "You want?" she asked in broken English.

"Yes."

She muttered to herself and turned away from him, stirring the pot, lifting thick chunks of vegetables with a small portion of the broth. Ned remained standing by the door. He felt at the knife tucked away under his pants. The side of it pressed into the fat of his ass, still dripping fresh blood. He made three quiet footsteps towards her.

She glanced at him, seeing his hand tucked behind his back. She frowned.

"Co?" She held up the small bowl of the soup.

Ned said nothing. She was only two steps away and an arm's length from thrusting the knife into her chest. Two steps and a single thrust from ever having to watch Eve bleed to death again.

He took a long breath.

"Matka, matka!"

Two girls burst into the room. One ran towards the soup and stood on her tippy toes, looking into the pot while the other pawed at the woman's cloak. They both wore simple dresses with flower prints, slippers a size too big for their little feet, clomping on the ground as they ran in. Their hair was black and held together with a tie decorated with a corn husk.

"Matka, jest gotowry?" the little girl said to the woman, tugging at her cloak again.

"Jestem glodny," the other girl said, standing by the soup, jumping up and down impatiently.

"Wkrótce," the woman said, staring at Ned. The two girls looked over, finally noticing him. The one closest to the woman took a step behind her while the other remained in open view by the soup pot, fidgeting, wishing she could hide as well without having to exert any effort.

"Lucja," the woman said, nodding towards the girl that stood alone. She wrapped a long arm around the other girl and kissed her head. "Dorata."

"You have daughters…" Ned took a step back. His hand still remained gripped upon the knife.

She nodded. "Uh… Lucy," she said, guessing the English equivalent. "And… uh, Darcy."

"Lucy and Darcy."

"Yes," she said, nodding. The girl standing by the pot took several steps closer to her mother and latched onto her leg. Both stared at him from behind the woman, using her like an old tree they could spy from. The woman held out the bowl of soup.

"Czerina," she said, offering the soup. "Black soup."

"No thank you," he said. He walked backwards. They stared at him as he crossed the threshold of the door, leaving it open. When he reached the truck he discretely pulled out the knife and set it down on the passenger side seat. Looking up, he found the moon behind a nylon of filthy sky, bright and yellow through the thick haze. It started to become dark as a dust storm approached them.

The wind began to howl.

There was a cry from the house.

The woman rushed out, holding the bucket. She presented it to Ned, shouting.

"Co to jest?" she shouted, lifting the bucket. A mouthful of blood spit out of the edge of the bucket on to the ground as she jerked it about. "What is this!?"

Ned covered his eyes as clods of dirt rushed past his face in a whirlwind that circled the house. He ran to the driver side of the truck and climbed inside, closing the windows.

The woman thrust the pale at him. The blood caught upon the storm of dust that had formed, turning it to rust. The air was bleeding out, covering the windows of the truck. Windshield wipers only smeared the bloody mess, making every view around him a massacre.

The woman continued to shout in her native tongue, her shrill voice carried by the wind. Ned started the truck and turned on his headlights. Only a faint yellow glow shined before him, worthless in the dust storm.

The limb of a dead tree shot through the driver's side window, shattering it and scraping his face as it flew out the passenger side. Hot blood fell from his face. Ned screamed.

The woman stood by the driver's side, fresh blood coated on her lips.

"Pig's blood!" she shouted at him, thrusting a finger.

He blindly felt for the knife. As the handle met his grip, he thrust his left hand out and grabbed the woman's neck. The two girls cried out from the house, their voices faint and shrill in the heavy wind. The storm grew worse.

"Matka!" they shouted.

"I'm sorry!" he screamed out, hoping the girls would hear him. "I'm so sorry!" He thrust the knife towards the woman's neck.

Her black eyes exploded with shock when the knife entered her throat. She shrank back, grinning in madness, blood spitting through her clenched teeth.

Her fingers twirled at him.

A tunnel of rust spun around the truck and it groaned and squealed as it was lifted off the ground. Soon enough, he was buried within the mouth of a storm and everything went black and he could not even hear himself as he begged and screamed for forgiveness.

§

Eve had stuffed herself. After dinner she had a big slice of cake and would've gone for seconds if her mother hadn't stopped her, saying she'd be up all night with a belly ache having nightmares when she should be resting up for chores the next day.

Her father wasn't around for the dinner. Right after he butchered the pig he told them he was gonna go see Harris about hiring some hands for a combine, hoping to maybe get a cheaper price if they went in on it together, saying he'd be late if they got to drinking. She hoped this meant that the wheat was dry enough to harvest and they wouldn't have to take her blood again. If she really had to, she'd let them do it. She was willing to do it earlier that day even when she hadn't eaten much and it made her afraid. It was hard to stop thinking about the dark empty field, running through it and slowly disappearing.

After helping her mother clean up the kitchen, she went upstairs and washed up for bed. A gentle storm had started up in the distance with flickers of white lighting. She pulled the covers up to her chin and watched it from her bedroom window, squinting on occasion when the flashes jumped from one cloud to another, sometimes striking the ground. Tufts of clouds slowly met one another, conspiring to bring about rain or hail.

Normally storms bothered her and she'd close the curtain at night as to not see whether or not a cloud was approaching her or passing her by. The heavy meal had calmed her, made her feel at ease as she watched the unfolding storm. It felt passive to her, as if it were happening on television instead of outside a thin sheet of glass.

Hail began to fall. Eve frowned. She was too young and had yet to learn everything there was to know about farming wheat, but she did know that hail could be bad, that under the right circumstances it could ruin a crop. She felt at the bump over her wrist, wondering if in a day or two her parents would approach her about making payment as they did every year, or maybe it would be too late and they'd lose everything. She couldn't pick a scenario that caused less distress and felt the knots in her stomach return, making her full belly ache. She laid flat on her back and tried not to move so that the pain would pass.

It was nearly dusk and the sun hid somewhere behind the prairie. The winds of the storm grew stronger, shoving all of the stalks of wheat to the ground. As Eve watched, her eyes grew heavy and she nearly fell asleep.

A skinny twister touched ground on the edge of the flat earth.

Eve sat up, staring at the window. All the color in her face quickly fell away.

It grew in size, collecting debris as it crawled towards them.

She stepped out of bed, standing closer to the window. The air felt like it was vibrating.

"Mommy," she said.

The twister grew closer, bigger. It was the color of rust, a twisting skeleton of freshly spilled blood.

"Mommy!" She started to shout, yet her body remained frozen, transfixed by the way the storm was alive, floating towards her in complete silence while chewing apart the ground beneath it, consuming all that it touched. There would only be seconds before it would reach her.

When it crawled over the outskirts of their backyard and loomed above the house, Eve couldn't help but notice the red pickup truck that was caught within the fibrous folds of the tornado's guts.

The headlights were still on.

The Cipher Sisters in: Saga Sideshow

Tone Baker

They stand at the edge of the potted road. Half an hour each, one stands one sits. The pair down to t-shirts in the unseasonable heat, looking on the lam for murder.

Aware their fortune is at a trickle, the sister at post attempts a ladylike ankle twist to extinguish her cigarette. Instead, she slips slightly on the butt and gasps in adrenal air, re-inhaling now stale smoke and stretching her mouth below her bottom teeth in a coughing fit to fight her own lungs. Her sibling stares at the landlocked fish at the sleeve of the highway, making an ass of herself with good and muddied heart. Scaring off the last visible automobile lights before the sun was completely gone. She invites her to change places, and let herself advertise.

Lucy no longer had her hand out. Sitting in the chirping black, one girl would hum low gibberish to assure her sister she was alive and aware. Not too loudly with chances of wolves around. Lucy heard gravel trampled down the road. Faint, but arriving. No headlight, but instead, two bug eyes of flashlight beams. Soon, the lights were on the sisters. Before getting too far, Darcy gave a short bark, to whoever drove the unlit vehicle. The flashlights aimed towards the rear of the automobile. A long train of accompanying cars and caravans halted behind.

The passenger door of the lead vehicle sprung outward. As younger sister for the moment Darcy was in mid-sneeze, her head met the door, and she reclined with a snotty groan of aching. The sharp man behind the wheel elbowed a smaller, bushier man in the chest. The stubby co-pilot patted the seat cushion beside him.

Entered Lucy, and on Lucy's knees was Darcy.

The plush driver spoke to the sisters. No English, but the girls hung on every word. The dwarven man beside them tilted his reflective head up, and informed them of the arrangement. Labor in exchange for travel, fair.

Lucy thumped her forehead into the back of Darcy's head, and Darcy nodded in agreement

The girls fell asleep fast. The slow ride would last until sun up. A juggling girl had stabbed a man in the last town. The band had become increasingly cautious after that.

The sisters woke in the care of elephants. The young lady nearby pitching hay onto the sleeping pair informed them to be wary of big movement. Plenty with the company had wrongfully aroused the elephants, and they'd hate to lose a set of twins to them.

They were pointed to the office of Boss Yodel, on the way being pulled by the employees to act as targets, safety nets, and reinforcement for a fistfight with an unhappy patron. Darcy took a balloon dart to the armpit.

Inside the boss' trailer, the small man is translating orders. The girls are to dress alike and mirror each other to pomp music. That afternoon Lucy was thrown into the circus band when their mirror act turned into a fight. Mister Yodel liked this better than his previous idea. The band was ordered to learn to take a punch.

Lucy and sister were sat on a horse trailer, drinking soft drinks quickly, throwing their bottles angrily on the ground. A young girl walks around the horse trailer. She's barefoot, there's cotton candy debris on her chin.

"You two are my sisters," she shouts, waning her feet on the crunchy ground.

Darcy dots the girl's nose with her big toe.

"My best trick is today," she tells them.

"Shirley Yupyup," shouts Lucy, "the last magician!"

Shirley skips away, glass scraping in the dirt.

Lucy wakes on the top of the horse trailer. She removes her glasses, brushing the sunburnt outline left on her face, and lashes obscenities into the air. There is a response to her shouting. Screams. Darcy is shaken awake, and the two rush towards the puff of smoke over the oddity house.

The smell is rotten close to the glow in the center of the crowd. Women and children screaming, terrified, but eager to see. It's Shirley Yupyup in a chair, on fire. Darcy vomits on a young boy standing in front of her.

After a tearful twin fistfight, the girls retire to their bunks. Sobbing and smearing make up and thin snot into their eyebrows. They slur small eulogies for the little sister between swallows of pocket whiskey. Sometime past midnight, they degrade into inviting the firemen clowns to their room to assault with thrown bottles.

The following week is smudged with lethargic performances. The sisters go noodle-armed and flail at one another until the weight of inebriation puts one of them to sleep. On sadder days, Darcy simply knocks out Lucy with her first strike. Lucy is forgiving.

That Sunday morning, Boss Yodel was sitting in their trailer. The sisters were unmoved by him being present during their sleep. "Boss needs to speak with you," said the stubby assistant, "alone." The four sat silent until the small man said to himself, "leave, Loragis," and proceeded to exit the trailer.

In a wonderful, rich, and broken English, the ringleader finally formally befriended the girls. "You two," he shook his finger, "should be dead one thousand times." The twins blushed a nauseous, half-drunken flush. "Girls from sideshows, miss their shows, to show up, to see your shows." They had figured that an internal betting parlor had given the performers more income than their daily show pay. No one wasted time with the mermaids, and fire-eaters when the twins were boxing.

"My me mother," continued Yodel, "paid for ticket." The boss' mother, in the past, would inform her son she was to feed herself to the lions. Mother Yodel would then change sweaters, and blend into the crowds. She wasn't refused free entry. She simply refused free entry. It made the most sense, or was funnier, to find a way in without paying.

"You kill me," cheered Yodel.

"Thank you," said Lucy.

"No," said Yodel with a stone drone, "you kill me. I. Kill I."

"I misunderstood, Lucy," said Darcy, "How funny are we?"

"Plenty," assured Lucy. The older sister for the moment, Lucy, left her bed, and knelt by the old man. "Are you saying," paced the worried twin, "what you think you're saying?"

The dwarf opened the door with a bully shoulder budge. "Mister Boss," he spoke mid tumble, "he wants to die." He would then brush the dust from his pants, and approach the kneeling girl with sincerity. "Help him."

"Shit," said Lucy.

That afternoon's performance was sloppy, and mumbling. Eventually the clowns would grab the girl's arms, and sling them towards each other. Soon the clowns couldn't retain their sadness either. Without context, the crowd began to hug and sob. An hour later the girls had a full trailer while celebrating the largest attendance since the circus's birth. Yodel was absent, his halfling right-hand topsy-turvy in the lap of the popcorn girl. "If we don't keep drunk," announced Darcy, "I believe we won't leave here alive."

"You're scared," yells Lucy, "I'm scared!"

The band with the bells of their horns protruding from the caravan window, shrieking a tipsy march. The dancing girls were rocking on chairs and tables to compete with the clowns straddling the remainder of the chairs and tables. The mobile home sexed its way into the mud, lop-siding party into the left-side wall. The cotton candy lady, who had been sitting in the kitchen's sink, was the only of the party not face down against the left interior of the tilting trailer. As the faucet that had been holding the madame broke loose, she cannonballed into the pile below. Before the cube crushed the grass beside it, Lucy recalled not having seen Yodel's man. Not him or the popcorn girl.

"They were making love in our top bunk," eulogized Darcy, "that's Lucy's bunk." She looked down to the lovers, comfortable sharing a single casket. "They rolled out of the window, our trailer rolled on them, and as we roll them into the ground, they will find rest in our hearts." After their pinebox was packed with popcorn to insure safe transport to the afterlife, they were lowered into the earth. Boss Yodel attended the reception, but demanded the trailer have its wheels removed. As to not repeat the crushing.

The twins performed an outrages amount of vomiting during the following show. Having been drunk for fifty one hours, the half hour show was the window of time where sobriety snuck in to hang them. Punch. Wretch. Splash. "Sorry." They would offer shoe cleaning to the audience, the audience politely declined. The fight ended with each sister falling asleep on the other's shoulder. Which was fortunate, since they were still projectile vomiting.

For the second time, they woke with the elephants. The animal's attendant hosed the spectrum of bile liquors from their clothing, the sisters still in them. Lucy began to fist fight the surge of water, shouting, "I can help you become a citizen!". Then more vomiting. Then more water. Darcy, still asleep, and ragdoll in the damp hay. Her sister, declaring her hate for the circus.

The candy apple girl was assigned to Darcy's bedside. Darcy exploded from comatose, grabbing the candy apple server by the neck and hair.

"Was it you!?," Darcy shook the concession ingenue.

"Apnapalapum hordeor," replied the candy apple girl, "nuckorn bopilopitamopola."

"I believe you," said Darcy, hugging the young lady. "Please fetch my sister, and the Juggling girl."

Baby Blue Jakes was celebrated for juggling dynamite. It was knives until knives weren't putting enough people in danger. She was no longer allowed to juggle them while lit without a scissors girl nearby. Extinguishing them in the mermaid tank had only put the mermaid in shock, and randomly throwing them killed people. She had collected guns throughout her lifetime, and didn't feel they were real weapons until they had actually taken a life.

"I need two pistols," ordered Darcy.

"For what," inquired Baby.

"Around $3.50," replied Darcy.

Outside of the boss' office the sisters stood with their handguns pointed at the door. Their faces were painted but running with Darcy's wailing. "I haven't got the stomach for this, Lucy," pleaded Darcy. "This isn't my idea," said Lucy. As her sister was poised to kick Yodel's door in, Lucy was promptly shit in the ass cheek. The shot girl lung forward headfirst, slamming the door open. Darcy was still kicking and extended her leg outward. The meat of her calf slapping her sister in the face. "Darcy," exclaimed Lucy, "my ass is bleeding, and we're under attack."

It was Boss Yodel who had shot the younger sister at the time. Most of his arguments were with the clowns, and had feared their mutiny Seeing the twins with their faces painted, and holding firearms, he had figured now was the time. Darcy stood up to see her sister's ass wound, still full of alcohol, she commenced vomiting. Boss and Darcy then assisted Lucy to her kitchen table, where the uninjured of the two proceeded to examine and pry out the bullet in the buttock. "I've done this before," beamed the surly surgeon, "a few times."

"I'm sorry, Mister Yodel," apologized Lucy between teeth gritting, "we can't kill you. We're not good in the business of other people."

Boss remained quiet. There was only circus music, and the scraping of tweezers on ass bone.

"I didn't think we'd have this many dead friends so soon," said Lucy. Passing a family sized bottle of rum to the candy apple girl, who would drink, and pass to Darcy. "I don't mind you reefer, candied apple girl," slurred Darcy, "but we are in enclosed space, and I've become jealous." She then pushed a rum soaked finger into the apple server's nose. "So skinny," Darcy's head thumped into the table, "With all that T, and all those apples. So skinny."

"Are we playing cards," asked Lucy, "I don't remember, but have clearly lost." She looked over to aware protege, "my sister is at rest, I will take that cigarette now."

Lucy dragged the poor girl around the carnival. Five times the candy apple girl had to wrestle the pistol from Lucy. Once when she shot a milk bottle at the milk bottle game in the midway. Once when she shot a balloon at the balloon dart game in the midway. Twice when they had ran out of cotton candy, and the last girl to receive one taunted Lucy by sticking out her tongue. Finally, when she shot the mirror the ladies restroom. The bullets were expended, and apple girl didn't have the energy to stop Lucy from brandishing the pistol. She had earned her brandishings.

When the twins woke, they were on a pile of apple cores, and informed that they had finished the days show hours ago. "We've done it again," said Lucy, "sleep brawling. I'd thought we'd gotten past this." Darcy tightened the knot on candy apple's bandana that held the beef muscle against her bruised eye. "You two will be alright," said their hurt nurse, "we keep waking up more hurt each day. It'll kill us."

"You're right, Bristles," said Darcy.

"My name is--"

"Apple girl," rose Lucy, "we speak to the staff today!"

"It's eight P.M.," moped apple girl, "they're too drunk already."

The sisters, and their apple hostess made way back to the home caravan. They would pass the busted lips, and makeup caking to cover the shiny skin beneath. The barkers, and sweet shop girls that used to lure with looks, now intimidated their patronage. Bad manners had gone from sultry and witty, to fightenous, and frightening. "We're going to leave behind killers," sighed Lucy, "we can't have that."

The congregation in the caravan took away few words that night. "Drink," and "fight," and "move your feet and drink," and "I'll shoot." Lucy was chewing the beef muscle from apple's eye, having felt purpose in the speech she had delivered. She had surely given the workers purpose, picked them up from the barbs of bad fortune. They were cheering the sisters louder than previous. The spirits had the room. The popcorn stand was on fire. "Shit," said Lucy.

The circus was banded around the popcorn dispensary, singing in solidarity. By the glow of fire that had met the butter bins in a blaze of passion and milk fat, the workers were at home. From the distance shouted Lucy. A simple drawn "NO!". If it harmonized beautifully with the singing circle, she may have been able to warn them better. She was tackled to the ground by the candy apple girl before the combustion.

Lucy cried as the swell of popping corn swallowed the mourning victims. Screaming to be released by her nurse. She would see the clowns sprayed in the face with unpopped kernels, only to have said kernels inflate, and latch to the sweat on those suffering faces. When the fire reached them, the corn burned on them like anniversary candles. The world of hurt before her that she could not help, and could never hope to. The salty dragon wandered as if alive, along the paths of those attempting to escape, and claw them into its hearth. Their leader ripped herself from the clutches of he caretaker, running into the angry wind that carry the ghoulish musk of burning kernels and brimstone.

By the time she reached the ones trapped under the popcorn's confectionery coal basin, they had been boiled alive my molten bars of butter. She would grab their arms only to be slurped back onto her bottom due to the coat of food spread on the crisping carrion. Though Lucy tried to clean the dairy death from her fingers with gasoline, they would feel a sickening slick many years from that day. The older sister at the time, Darcy, picked up her delirious and screaming sibling, and rocked her gently as she walked back to their mobile home.

"I'm pretty sure," dazed a heartbroken Lucy, "that everywhere we go isn't like this." She began to cry into milk, "people do not erupt into flames after having charity extended to them! Where is where our path went wrong?"

"Funnier still," said Darcy, "we have not seen a single police officer since we've arrived."

"Girls," entered candy apple girl, "people aren't staying. They're turning around as soon as they exit their vehicles. I think the bodies are running them off."

"We've got nowhere to bury them," argued Lucy, "and no one to help with the burials. It's just me, you and Darcy here."

"And Boss Yodel," informed Darcy.

"Boss Yodel," said Lucy, "Shit."

They found their boss with his office door open, holding a wine decanter and a rifle. The three survivors knelt at the cuff of his robe. "When they give you the circus," he mooned towards his weapon, "they say 'this circus will kill you, be sure not to kill it before then.'"

Lucy hung her head, wine would be spilt in her hair because of this.

"We were never great," whined Boss, "we were alive, though. Then. All alive. Most of our teeth. Alive."

In the fields, there were vultures at the dead, and crows at the corn. The crows were also at the dead, but exclusively at the corn. None happy about being shooed away from meals, the buzzards would challenge the twins and the candy apple girl. Darcy began to shoot the birds that weren't agreeable.

The bodies were pulled from under corn, and rested in rows. "I don't supposed," suggest candy apple, "we lie them in the crater around the popcorn monument."

"It would grow some great corn," said Darcy, "however, I think there's a more dignified way to put our friends to rest."

Within the hour, the girls had assembled and placed the entirety of their fallen family into the carnival high swing. "Activate the machinery," barked Darcy. The riders soared once again. Their distant faces almost seemed to smile back to the girls. The mighty swing was issuing the departed into the sunrise. Cozy in their seats, some holding dead buzzards for companions. Lucy felt back in the trailer, becoming loud and dizzy with the crowd, waving to them as the rushing wind lifted their arms. She was lost in the feeling, and was delivered a boot into her face.

The boot was still with foot, and had been launched from one of the seats above them. In no time, many things were flying from their old friends way. Arms, burnt candy, costume jewelry, entrail deposit, miscellaneous guts, and glitters. "Mistake," said Lucy, trying not to open her mouth too wide, "turn it off, Darcy! Darcy, turn it off!"

Darcy halted the machine with its patrons still suspended in air.

"We've done it," said Lucy, "we've killed most of this circus, and it's only going to correct our good deeds if we kill Yodel too."

"Well," said Darcy, "I'm out of ammunition. He may shoot back this time."

"He's already shot back," strained Lucy, adjusting her seat.

In the trailer of the late Baby Blue Jakes, they found Baby Blue cursing them. "It's too fucking early," she shouted, followed by a large glass bottle hurled and making contact with the candy apple girl. Then cursed candy apple, and began the exchange of unbroken glass between the three girls and the angry juggler. "Jakes," yelled candy apple, "I'm going to eat your fucking eye!"

"Oh," gasped the juggler, "it's you guys."

"Baby Blue," groaned Lucy, "why weren't you at the fire last night?"

"I don't even like popcorn," protested Baby.

"There weren't any survivors," informed Darcy.

"Well, shit," said Baby Blue, "am I good to go back to sleep then?"

"The circus is gone," cried Lucy, "there's nothing left! It's over!"

"It's been over," barked Baby Blue, smacking Lucy's bloody forehead, "even fucking Yodel knows. That's why he picked you outsiders to kill him."

"Huh," gulped Darcy.

"And you didn't even do that right," scolded Jakes, "do you know how many people are looking to kill him?"

The twins shook their heads in stupidity.

"A lot," boomed Baby, "the clowns, who are dead now, but still. The popcorn girl kept putting scorpions in his popcorn bags, until somebody told that dumbass that they were his favorite. Little half guy thought if he killed the boss he'd become him, kept asking his permission."

Darcy stood firing her empty gun at the ground and wobbling on the ball of her foot.

"You had one job," belittled Baby Blue, "you perform your bullshit act for a few days, kill Yodel, and leave. The circus was broke, and we were all on our own after the season. Yodel has a dead carnival, and you can't even accidentally get this guy dead!"

The sisters, and their nurse left the trailer with heavy conscience, full ammunition, and runny noses. They shamefully walked in the unattended tall grass, crunchy with the blood from the last night's disaster.

"I'm going to do it," said the candy apple girl in triumph, "I'll step into his office and do it. He won't know it wasn't you two."

"No," Lucy ran after her, "no, no, no!"

The treat serve began to sprint towards Yodel's home. "I'm going to make all of this right," she fanfared in dash, "he'll be so proud! He'll love me! He'll call me by my name! He'll hug and hold me before he's fully dead! It's happening. It's happening now."

The twins couldn't meet the girl's zeal, spirit, speed, or enthusiasm. "It doesn't work that way," Lucy begged from behind her heels, "It doesn't work that way! He does not want that!"

"No," candy apple girl soared over the scraping vegetation, broken glass, and unpopped kernels, "this is exactly what he wants! I have to do this! It was always supposed to be me!"

Lucy wasn't going to make it to the dangerously delusional girl by she met the porch of Boss Yodels caravan. She raised her gun in the air and fired her chambers empty. "Julip Yodel! Get your ass back here! Right! Now!"

Candy apple girl hesitated at the door. She gave an apologizing look to the out of breath sister, still dragging her feet towards her. "Daddy," she cheered as she flung the mobile home's door open. The door handle was caught on some twine. The twine was tugging at a working mess of wooden bars and pulleys. Finally, the twine ended, tied with a tight bow onto the trigger of Boss Yodels hunting rifle. Candy apple girl was ejected from the door way. Lucy wearily caught the flying sweet shop girl, and they tumbled beside one another.

"Boy," choked the Yodel daughter, "is my face red."

"Shit," said Lucy.

There hadn't been much noise in the next few hours. The birds had been scared off by Darcy killing most of them. The popcorn was going to waste, and began to be strewn about the rare and bloody fair ground. The carts of the Ferris wheel gave in, and smashed the remainder of concession stands. "It's not fair," huffed Darcy, "it's not fair at all. I like making new friends, I do. If this is going to be the pattern though, I don't feel like I was formed to be friendly."

"It's not always this bad," cooed Lucy, "it's not normally this bad. This isn't normal. None of this is happening in this manner anywhere in the world. We'll be in the rest of the world soon. I believe we've had enough stupid in our socks to get us to our gray days."

"I've even liked the god damned circus," panted Darcy.

"No shit," said Lucy.

They had been long napping in mister Yodel's office when his automobile arrived. Darcy had been resting on the rifle mechanism, and Lucy with her feet on Darcy's head. The ancient ring leader set a paper grocery bag on the kitchen table between the girls. "Friend or foe, Yodel," the older sister at the time demanded. "Come with I," shook their boss.

In a tent the girls had never been in, or seen built, and was immaculately cleaner than all other areas of the circus considered, Boss Yodel stood in front of a large glass basin. From his large paper bag he produced a large glass bottle. "More liquor," asked Darcy, "I can't. I could. I shouldn't."

"Corrosive," said Boss Yodel.

"Oh," said Lucy, "I see."

After the tub was filled, Yodel disrobed, and offered his hand to Lucy. The girl was a baby again, red in the face, mucus to her chin, and babbling with her cry convulsions. The old man entered sizzling feet first, he adjusted himself, and reclined with the liquid up to his chest. There was no alarm in his face, no change in voice while he was still able to speak, not a glance into the past calamities. Just gratitude. Naked, dissolving gratitude. For all the bad they had done, they did good.

"Do you think," quivered a bawling Darcy, "it hur--"

"Of course it fucking hurts," sniffed Lucy.

Leaving the boss to his final rest, they exited the tent. Lucy looking back, "Goodbye Mister Yodel," she said. "I'll never-- Christ! That is fucking gross. Why is the tub clear?"

Outside, the sister met the scenery before them. The broken machines, the people on them, the tipped caravans, and the drifting popcorn. A mess. Just like them. A happy mess. Just like them.

"I let ALL the animals out," roared Baby Blue Jakes taking one of the trailer trucks, "you should probably get out of here. There were a lot of lions!"

The girls quickly found the ignition keys to Boss Yodel's vehicle. In their rearview, more rides fell on more midway stands. The standing carnival receded into the popcorn crater, never to be found again. After 30 miles of cry-driving, they had found the highway.

"Where do we go from here," asked Darcy.

"We have an apartment," said Lucy.

"Oh. Fuck! Did we leave the pets enough food?"

"Shit," said Lucy.

Mickey Slim
Chris Deal

In the town of El Dorado, there were two moderately known citizens, Lucy and Darcy. The stories about those twins could be enough to fill a book, though the truth in regards to anything when it comes to those two could rarely be verified. What was known, though they spent their lives solely in the company of each other after the death of their parents, was that Lucy fell in love in the summer of 1959. The two girls had just turned twenty and when they walked the streets of El Dorado arm in arm, no one thought a mirage had risen up through cracks in the pavement. They were not beautiful girls, though never were they offensive to the eyes, but no poet dedicated a single word to them girls.

The object of Lucy's desire was one Richie R. Hoagland, a salesman of high-grade insecticides from New Mexico. Tall as a cornstalk and near as lean, no one in El Dorado knew him save for what came from his own lips. He was a desert rat and claimed to have been present when the ship crashed through the farmland outside of Roswell. The girls were just out of their teens and Richie was pushing thirty.

They met him at the beginning of that summer, at Zbyszko's Cafeteria, the small diner where each was a waitress. Their name tags alone were all that could differentiate the two when they were in their uniforms, save for a freckle in the shape of a crescent moon on the soft of Darcy's neck. Lucy was smitten, though Darcy was not taken in by his attempts at charm. Lucy loved his eyes, the way the grayness sparkled with flecks of gold in the light of day, as well as his smile, which curved exactly like the horizon.

Richie was in town trying to woo the area's farmers to invest in the various concoctions he carried around in his leather briefcase, such as endosulfan and dichlorodiphenyltrichloroethane, which had been shown in 1939 to be effective in preventing the spread typhus and malaria, as well as being able to thwart the destruction of crops from them vile insects that went around looking for a free meal. He was partial to a glass of gin with a dash of DDT in the evenings.

Every morning he would set up shop at the diner, where he would charm Lucy and work his way among those closest to the town with the morning ritual of imbibing Zbyszko's coffee each. After the morning rush he would venture out into the fields that lined the earth around El Dorado, coming back around during dinner hours. He had a batch of the best insecticides money could buy and could talk his way into anyone's house for a glass of tea or a roll in the hay.

Richie and Lucy's time together began with a trip to the cinema three towns over. She was thrilled to have something uniquely her own, as she had grown up around the poverty line, having to share most of her life with her sister. Darcy's eyes blackened each time Lucy returned from a date with Richie. Darcy thought of herself as the older, more mature twin and had made it her goal to protect her sister, though whether her motives were purely altruistic cannot be known, nor what really happened after Lucy convinced Darcy to come to dinner with her and Richie one evening in late July. What is known is Richie R. Hoagland was not seen again around El Dorado. Word that went around at first held he skipped town without delivering any of the various insecticides he had promised to deliver. It came with the discovery some weeks later of a burned out husk of a car out in the wilds beyond the fields that the story started to change, little by little with each new telling, like a memory being reconstructed each recollection.

The way the story is told now is that Darcy, eager to find any reason to hate Richie, noticed when they went for dinner that there was a bit of skin on his left ring finger that was significantly lighter than the rest of his fingers. It was in the shape of a perfect circle. She continued conversing politely with Lucy and her beau, and even offered to get him his choice of drink. The DDT was supplemented with a little something extra from Richie's bag of tricks, they say. Richie was noticeably woozy when the trio left that night, heading towards the outskirts of town. Each speaker, having grown up in El Dorado and finding Lucy and Darcy something close to local, living landmarks, stopped short of finishing the story, being that only they know what happened that night, though the story holds a kernel of truth in that, following her brief tryst with Richie R. Hoagland, Lucy was considerably more sour in her disposition, while Darcy always kept a small smile with her.

You and Me
Adam Autin

Sun and pond seared silver together, a shimmering haze broken into a series of circles leading toward the shore. From sand, figures rose. From hands, stones skipped. The symmetry of throws fit twin girls.

A matching set in pale flesh and paler nightgowns, their identical ideal was marred by a mere detail: whereas light weaved a luminous golden glow into Lucy's boyish locks, Darcy's closely cropped darkness absorbed all and returned none. In the passing of a cloud, even that slight divergence slipped away.

Darcy courted a shiver in the momentary shade. Lucy reached for another stone, but found only pretender pieces from a broken bottle. The girls looked at each other in full knowledge of who would go. Darcy came down, like the returning sun, upon a large white rock. The water lay still in wait.

Lucy climbed through the reeds. Darcy receded. Lucy brushed past the tall grass. Darcy fell farther back. Sticking to the outskirts of the pond, Lucy scoured for sand and smooth stones. Another cloud darkened the world. With it, a breeze blew a shiver through Lucy. The shiver deepened with the whine that followed. The breeze gone, the cloud moved on, Lucy looked back upon the whine and its root: a shadow shrinking toward the pond to escape growing shadows ever encroaching.

The tall grass whipped at her flesh as Lucy ran. The reeds tore at her gown. Faster, faster. Her hair struck a bright golden flame across the sky. Forgoing the physical, Lucy gave in to speed. She was an indistinguishable figure in the light.

Lucy stopped running only when she came to Darcy–her back to the pond, legs limp against the white rock, trembling red hands holding waning support in the sand. Scattered sticks and stones outlined her fallen form in a savage picture frame. Above it all, the desperate whine drew and burst like a siren.

Lucy looked upon the cause: three wild beasts–dirty, unkempt, laden with natural weapons from trees and earth. These older boys, terrors along country roads. These older boys, taken over by instinct and impulse. These older boys, threats to the fragile peace Lucy kept safe for Darcy. With a growl, Lucy imagined herself one of these beasts.

The boys thought it best to flee when the snarling little girl in the tattered nightdress barreled down on them like a feral animal. Implements and attitudes dropped with the same suddenness. They did not escape unscathed. Scrapes and scratches adorned their retreat and would serve as future reminders to avoid the twin girls whispered about but rarely seen.

She exhaled as she folded into Darcy. Darcy melted with tearful moisture into Lucy. The whine muffled itself within the stifling closeness. Bits of broken bottle were brushed from bloodied palms. Red streaked down the white rock. Darcy burrowed her face deeper into Lucy. Lucy inhaled as her heart pushed into Darcy.

Eyes burning, Lucy bit her lip and grasped at glass. Burn gave way to flood, skin turned slick. She pushed staining fingers toward the ruined rock. Fresh blood mixed with bad. Her fingertips formed two broken triangles. From the apices, she drew parallel lines to heaven, joining them with a violent slash. Atop it all, she formed two circles, like two vibrant and thriving suns.

Lucy brushed a dented lip to the ear at her chest with another spoken secret heard only by Darcy: "It's you and me."

That's Showbiz

Jason Matthews

"And now, our trumpet player, Miss Harriet Shue, has written a loverly Mexican mariachi song all about yours truly, Spade Cooley. So let's give a big hand to Harriet and the loverly Miller Twins."

He sounds like he's buying pork chops at the market, thought Darcy Miller as Harriet blasted the opening rip.

He sounds like he's about to pass out in the corner, thought Lucy Miller as the bassist thumped in.

"Big smiles," said Darcy.

"Left foot first," said Lucy.

The sisters squeezed hands quickly and stepped from the wings.

§

"It's falling apart," said Darcy, as the taxi made a left onto Santa Monica. "Last week with the calypso number; this week, mariachi. What's next? 'Spade Cooley's All-Girl Rock 'n' Roll Revue'?"

"That's showbiz, hon," said Lucy.

"How can you be flip about this? These are our careers!"

"This is us earning some summer pin money."

"Darling, the first time we did the show, Mr. Cooley had seventy-five percent of the viewers in Los Angeles—"

"—Which was about a thousand people—"

"So? The show was bigger than Milton Berle!"

"We were ten. We bought a bunch of candy and ate until we got sick. I didn't see you nose-deep in a copy of Variety."

"Don't you want to be famous?"

"No. I want to have a nice, quiet life. Maybe a dog, too."

"Well, I want more."

"That's nice. It's good to want things."

"I want to audition for Lawrence Welk."

"I'm sure Marty would be glad to set that up, so long as he gets his ten percent. Knock 'em dead, hon."

"But I want you to audition, too!"

"No, thank you. I'd like to spend the last summer of my high school career not hustling for work."

"Please, Lulu? Pretty please? I'll be your very best friend."

Lucy sighed. If she didn't relent, Darcy's next tactic would be baby talk. Anyway, what could it hurt? Welk already had the Lennon Sisters, and there were four of them. Lucy doubted he'd need an extra matching pair of eighteen-year-olds on the payroll.

"Set it up."

§

Marty Green's office was just off Cahuenga. He ran his liver-spotted hands through what remained of his hair and looked across at the twins.

"I just got off the phone with Don Swenson, Welk's producer," he said. "He says he's wild about you girls. 'Get 'em down here straight away!' he said."

"Well, great!" said Darcy. Lucy refrained from rolling her eyes. Marty lit a Chesterfield and leaned back.

"There's just this thing. You know about Welk, right?"

"What about him?"

"Well–how strict are your parents about things? Chores, homework, clothes? Boys? Either of you have a boyfriend?"

They blushed in tandem.

"Okay, so that's a no. But do your folks expressly forbid it?"

"No," said Darcy.

"We just haven't met the right--"

"No need to explain," interrupted Marty, raising his hands. "You should know, though, that Welk considers himself head of his own little Musical Family. He's got a morality clause built into his contracts and he's real serious about it." He held up his cigarette. "These, for example. Welk sees you with one of these; you're out on your sweet patooties."

"We don't smoke," said Lucy.

"Nor will you, if you get the job. No skirts higher than mid-shin in public, no salty language, and if you meet boys, the show insists on vetting them. If they don't pass muster, they're gone. I've seen kids much younger than you go spare trying to live under these kinda restrictions–it's only natural–so I want you to really think about whether you can do it."

"Absolutely," said Darcy, faux gravitas behind each syllable. Lucy glared at her. Marty looked between the two and shook his head.

§

They auditioned at the Palladium, where Welk's show was filmed. Neither of them could see into the gloom beyond the footlights. For all they could tell from the stage, they were performing "Tonight, You Belong to Me" to a completely empty house. Still–raven hair pin-curled and swept-back, dresses a bit frillier than usual, just enough makeup to pick out their eyes and not shine under the lights, and Big Smiles–they laid the wholesomeness on as thick as they dared.

Lucy held the last chord on her ukulele until its tones completely vanished from the room.

"Thank you, ladies," came a man's voice from the back of the room. He sounded about as enthusiastic as a proctologist on his tenth patient of the day. "We have your information."

Darcy and Lucy left the stage, showbiz smiles frozen on their faces until they were safely out of sight. Lucy turned to her sister.

"Well, I certainly got the 'just wild about us girls' feeling. Didn't you?"

§

"Great news!" said Darcy, as she barged into Lucy's room the following Tuesday. "The Lennon Sisters are going on tour next week. Marty says the Welk Show wants us at rehearsals next Monday! They're sending over the contracts now!"

Lucy felt a headache coming on. She'd been looking forward to a quiet week: A trip to the library, maybe take in that new Astaire picture with Cyd Charisse. Now Darcy would be pestering her to practice.

They'd been performing since they were six. Granted, it had its moments, and she loved seeing Darcy happy when things were going well, but she was tired of all the work that went into getting ready to do the work of looking for work that was ultimately just... work. She was pretty sure that most of the other kids in their class didn't do summer jobs where you had to practice flipping burgers on your off-hours, or drill babysitting routines until you wanted to actually sit on the baby in question.

But she flashed Darcy a quick smile and said, "That's wonderful, hon."

§

Rehearsals were tricky. Everyone else knew each other; knew what was expected of them. The sisters took their cues as best they could, but Welk saw Darcy put a wink at the end of "Get Happy".

"None of that, now," he said. "This is a song about preparing to meet the Maker, not preparing to meet a sailor."

"Don't fret, girls," said Alice Lon, Welk's "Champagne Lady," after the man had walked off to deal with another detail of the show. "He once docked me for doing the Charleston at a party. He's a decent fellow, but he's a bit stiff."

§

Saturday, the night of the show, and Lucy couldn't find Darcy anywhere backstage. She finally tried the alley behind the venue and heard the familiar trill of her sister's laugh–so much more vital than her own, she thought–coming from around the corner.

Then she heard smacking sounds–kissing sounds–and crept quietly to peek.

Darcy was there, in a green taffeta outfit that matched Lucy's, shoes like Lucy's, hair done up exactly like Lucy's. However, unlike Lucy, she was locked in a passionate clinch with Harriet Shue, the trumpeter from Mr. Cooley's band.

Her eyes wide, Lucy stifled a squeak with both hands and quickly retreated. Before she had time to process, though, light washed in from the other end of the alley and the familiar sound of a camera's flash echoed. Darcy and Harriet shrieked, and Lucy dove behind some pallets as they came running past in heels.

§

A runner brought them straight from the stage to Don Swenson's office, Lucy still clutching her ukulele. The producer was holding an 8x10, fresh out of the developing bath.

"Well, girls? Which one of you is this?"

Darcy stared at the photo like a rabbit under the glare of oncoming headlights. Lucy could see her sister's dreams of fame and fortune swirl down the toilet. She took a breath.

"Me, sir," she said, ignoring Darcy's gasp.

"I was afraid of that. We might've been able to use you and your ukulele as a solo act. Well, I hope you're proud of yourself. Your moral degeneracy has cost you and your sister this job. If your behavior should, at any time in the future, be tied to Mr. Welk, I will see to it that you never work again. Please see yourselves out."

§

Darcy knocked on Lucy's door as she was getting ready for bed. Lucy sat down on the mattress and motioned for her sister to join her. Darcy sat, hands folded in her lap. When she spoke, her voice was barely a whisper.

"Thank you, Lulu," she said.

"I wish I'd known, hon," said Lucy. It took a moment to phrase the next part: "Do you... love Harriet?"

"I don't know. I don't think so. She's got strong lips."

"Trumpet player."

"Yeah."

Darcy broke into sobs. Lucy cradled her sister, rocking slowly back and forth.

"Lulu?" she said, when she could catch her breath.

"Yeah, hon?"

"A quiet life sounds good, right about now."

"Yeah."

"I don't want a dog, though."

"Okay."

Mercy

Rebecca L. Brown

Sure I remember them! They were the bonniest little things I'd ever seen. Went everywhere together, if they could get away with it; them and that dog-eared old rag-doll of theirs. The day she went missing we thought we'd never hear the end of it!

When was this? Oooh, now that's a good question. It was the year that 'Near You' by Francis Craig was in the charts. Either forty seven or eight, I think. They were nine at the oldest, but no younger than seven. Lovely polite little girls, they were. Always remembered their manners when they came to the shop--I worked in that shop for near sixty years, you know. Never would have left if it wasn't for my bad ankles. Both swollen up like balloons these days. I'll show you if you like… If you have the time…

No?

Where was I? Ah! The little doll…

We put up a 'Missing' poster for her, of course. In the shop. Even offered a reward for information, just like a real 'Missing' poster does. It was a small town, mind, and anyone who found her would know she was theirs. Like I say, they always had her with them. They held her between them, one hand each, as if she was the third sister. They used to call her 'Mercy', if I remember rightly. Talked to her sometimes and paused to wait as if she answered them back, only the rest of us couldn't hear.

Mercy turned up right after they moved away. Funny how when you stop looking everything just seems to turn up like that. Harry Jones found her caught up in the branches of an old tree and brought her into the shop to see if we could find a way to send her on to them. We couldn't, though. They didn't leave a forwarding address with anyone, so far as I know.

Mercy looked pretty sorry for herself when they found her, of course; must have been there for weeks and she was well-loved even before that. One of her felt eyes was missing and the fabric was soaked through, going moldy in places.

I fixed her up nicely--even gave her a new hat with a flower on it--and sat her in the corner of the shop on a little chair. Miss Mercy stayed there until I retired, then she came with me.

Do you think you could give Mercy back to them, maybe? It's only I reckon they'd love to see her after all this time... It's funny how much you treasure the old things when you're running out of time for new ones.

1971

Ken Goudey

Darcy wandered between the slot machines. Her hand clutched a small stack of half dollar coins--John Kennedy's profile pressed into her sweaty palm. She pretended to search for just the right one-armed bandit, but in truth she sized up the men gambling away their dignity--a search she would repeat many times in the ensuing years. She approached an inviting machine, two away from the short man in a brown coat and derby, chewing on a disgusting cigar, and snapped her coin into the slot.

She yanked the lever and stared at the spinning wheels.

§

Three months earlier she had sat on the dressing room counter in the back of a small theater in Orange County. Her peach-toenails barely extended past the large flutes of her polyester jumpsuit, her dark curls lay perfectly in place, her scarf hung around her neck with a precise knot. She twirled a cigarette in her fingers. Lucy sat in the next chair, brushing mascara through her lashes.

"I don't want to go." Darcy flicked her lighter and inhaled deeply. The twins never argued. Never an impasse. Only ever the road not taken.

"I don't want to be a sideshow anymore." Lucy held her lower lid and glanced at her sister for a moment. "What did the gypsy say?" She matched the liner on her eyes to Darcy's.

Darcy exhaled across the tip of her cigarette. "That you'll die before me."

"Hardly." Lucy shook her head and nodded towards the glowing tip in Darcy's hand. "What did she really say?"

"That we shouldn't trust strangers. That we'll never leave if we go. That the road untraveled is a dangerous thing." She drew again at her cigarette. "At least that's what I got out of it. She really wasn't making sense. I think she might have been high on something."

"They're all drunks." Lucy put down her pencil and produced a silver half dollar, which she balanced on her thumb, ready to flip. "The road not taken?"

§

The wheels landed on two sevens and a cherry, and the machine began spitting out fifty half dollars.

"Whoo-wee!" The man in brown exclaimed around his cigar. His name was Cyrus, though Darcy would never know. "Ain't that a thing!"

Darcy smiled, but didn't turn. 'Let him watch,' she thought and pulled a cigarette from her purse. He was right there with a light.

She took her time and felt the smoke ease her nerves. "Thank you." She still didn't make eye contact. Play it timid. Concentrate. She pulled one of the coins from the tray as soon as the racket stopped and plugged it back into the slot. She gave the lever a jerk and drifted off as the wheels spun once more.

§

The snow crunched beneath Darcy's shoes as she walked along the shore. Across the icy, still surface of the lake a man in a rowboat made his way towards the casinos. She stared until he disappeared into the darkness and the cold cut through her wool coat, then turned back towards the cabin.

"How will we be compensated?" Darcy's words were visible for an instant as she closed the door - the chill inside her evident as she spoke.

The Washoe named Steve remained on the floor, atop the buckskin he had brought, and stared into the deep blue-green flames that enveloped the large log in the hearth. Other than the skin, and a beaded necklace, Steve looked like a large, Mexican cowhand, which had been a particular disappointment for Lucy. The other man, younger, small, and balding, with wire-rimmed glasses and an anxious personality, perched on the edge of their couch. He wore an imprudent quantity of native garb and claimed 'Cloudsong' was his name. His ignored whiskey created a sweat ring on their coffee table.

"There's no, erm, paycheck, if that's what you mean. Things will just work out. You catch my drift?" Cloudsong tried to make his words sound poetic.

Darcy settled on the edge of the hearth, careful not to block Steve's view of the burning log. "Not really. What if we decide to quit?"

Lucy clanked something hard in the kitchen.

Cloudsong shook his head. "No, Man, it just doesn't..."

Steve looked up into Darcy's eyes. "Once you make this connection, there can be no unmaking it. Da'aw will provide all you need, and you, pay through obligation."

Darcy held his gaze. "Then would you do it?"

Steve paused, his eyes drifting from Darcy to the window, then nodded and turned back to the fire. A chant began to spill over his lips-- words even he had never before heard.

§

Bar...Blank...Cherry. The machine stopped with an unceremonious ka-chunk. Darcy bit her lip and smiled as she fished for another coin in the tray. She could feel his eyes on her every move, though he pretended to rediscover interest in his own machine. She dropped the coin in, took a drag on her cigarette, and pulled the lever one final time.

§

Lucy pushed at her thin, drawn hips. She was gaunt and stretched. She shook when she tried to be still. Darcy hadn't withered nearly as fast, but felt the hunger in the lake eating away her insides. The spring thaw had brought with it a longing like neither had ever experienced nor expected. No communication had come from Steve, or Cloudsong, in nearly three months, nor would it ever.

"I can't take this." Lucy lay curled up by the back door, staring at the lake. "I didn't realize..." She couldn't finish the thought, but Darcy knew exactly what occupied her mind.

"Nor did I, but, I don't see any choice." Darcy stood at the counter and forced herself to eat the rejected bowl of Cream of Wheat she had prepared for Lucy, despite the fact that the very idea repulsed her. "Just try to spruce up a bit. You look a little like a gargoyle."

§

Darcy felt her stomach cramp. Cherry...Cherry...Cherry. The machine erupted once more, enthusiastically beginning the delivery of twenty more half dollars.

"Darlin', you got the touch." Cyrus now stood at her side, watching her machine spit coins and coveting Darcy's luck even more than her beauty. She turned her eyes up to meet his and smiled. She twirled her hair and spoke sweetly, initiating the process of taking him home.

The front door banged open and Cyrus stumbled into the hallway. He propped one shoulder against the wall, his drunken eyes seeing a double Lucy at the end of the hall. He laughed, then slapped his knee.

"She said she had a sister, but I'll be dammed if you ain't her spittin' image!" He twisted to see Darcy, who smiled, giggled, and before he could turn back, Lucy closed and landed a heavy skillet on his brainpan, knocking the half-eaten cigar out the front door.

§

The sisters struggled to drag the flaccid, corpulent, naked, and unconscious man down to the beach from their cabin. The first rays of dawn painted copper streaks high in the black skies as their feet finally dipped into the freezing, clear water. Darcy prayed the cold wouldn't revive him, and, to her surprise, he slept as he floated on the surface. Thigh-deep and shaking with cold, they gave a gentle push and slogged back to the shore where they sat on either side of the rut they had made in the sand.

"Now what?" Darcy could feel her sister concentrating as she stared at the fat belly floating on the surface. Then in an instant something coiled around him and he was gone.

"Next time, get a thinner one." Lucy dropped her head into her hands, then snickered.

"Next time?" Darcy felt the light in her soul returning rapidly--the fire at her core restored. She knew Lucy was feeling the same. "You're going next time."

Lucy produced a half dollar from her pocket and propped it on her thumb. "The road not taken?"

Regular Earharts

Andrew McElrath

Marco had always made good coffee. He was a scoundrel and unapologetic fascist, but it was enough that Lucy could stand to bear his company.

"They cultivate them in Brazil, you know. I've seen the fields. It's quite beautiful."

She held the cigarette to her temple, a practiced interest in her expression. She no longer needed to remind herself to nod at the end of his sentences. Nothing Marco said ever stuck, but she let him have his moments. Stirring her coffee, she smiled, warmly, excusing herself.

Even on mornings such as this, Darcy preferred to keep to herself. Her eggs were scrambled, burnt, the coffee medium grade at best, but serviceable. She chewed quietly at a piece of toast as Lucy returned, crumpling the unused cigarette in the ashtray.

"He offered you another one?"

"He always does."

"He'll have to run out one of these days."

"Somehow I don't think he will."

"Hmmm."

Lucy looked up to her sister.

"So gloomy today. It's your birthday. Couldn't hurt to smile a little, could it?"

"It's your birthday too."

"That's beside the point. Come on, buck up."

Darcy hesitated, before trying her best.

"…Well, we'll have time to work on that. Got something special planned for today."

"Safe, I should expect."

"Safe…er."

"…Er?"

A prolonged sip was all that answered her.

The farm itself proved a short breath from the apartment block, only a couple of minutes by the car Darcy refused to let her sister drive, delegating Lucy to navigation. A sparse wind sent a ripple through the passing fields, and out front of the house and the barn stood a young girl in a yellow dress and a stern expression, an aviator's cap pushed up on her forehead, a large sunhat in her hand.

"Been expecting you. You're late."

"Excuse me?" Darcy exited the vehicle, wincing, shielding her eyes from the sun.

"Mama said to dock your pay if you were late again. Papa thought likewise."

"I'm sorry, I have no idea what you're talking about."

"Darcy, please," Lucy exited from the passenger side. "I'll handle this."

The girl's expression wavered a little.

"Lucy? That you?"

"I'm here, I'm here. This is my sister, Darcy. I've mentioned her before, I'm sure."

"Told me you had a sister. Didn't think it was that kind of sister."

"Yes, well, the cat's out now I'm afraid. And Darcy, this is Addie."

"Addie?"

"That's Adeline Fitzgerald to strangers, stranger."

"…Of course. It's…nice to meet you, Adeline."

"Fitzgerald."

"…Adeline Fitzgerald."

"Addie, where are your parents?"

"Out. Why I'm standing here waiting for you." Adeline removed the aviator's cap, and handed it to Lucy. "The Bird's out back, where it always is."

"Ah, good. Darcy, would you kindly?"

Behind the barn sat a scrap hangar, where a modest aircraft awaited them. WWI in make, refurbished, converted for crop dusting. Lucy turned, presenting it with a little flourish. Darcy stopped dead in her tracks.

"An airplane?"

"The Bird! The name is a little on the plain side, but it doesn't seem to mind too terribly much."

"You can fly an airplane?"

"Well, yes. After a fashion. Mr. Fitzgerald's a better teacher than he gives himself credit for."

Lucy flashed a smile. Darcy was still adding things up.

"You mean to tell me all those days you-"

"Yes, yes."

"Do you even have a license?"

"Not exactly. It's sort of an under the table arrangement."

"Why are you showing me this?"

"Well, it's your birthday."

"Our birthday."

"Our birthday. Would you like a ride?"

Darcy recoiled a few paces, her expression muddled, closely guarded apprehension mixed with the unexpected onset of longing.

"Remember when you—-when we—-were six? Said you wanted to fly. Like a bird in the sky. Like father in the wars, though not IN the wars, particularly. Well?"

Darcy approached the aircraft, running her hand cautiously over its body. She tapped and felt the front propeller, turning it slightly. It was some time before she turned back to her sister.

"…Alright."

The cockpit had had been enlarged, lengthened, made for two, though it was still quite cramped.   There was something about the noise it made as it took off that gave Darcy pause, but Lucy assured her it was nothing.

"Aaaaand here we are."

They soared only a few dozen feet, maintaining close comfort to the ground, but it didn't matter.   Lucy smiled at her sister's own wonderment.

"Is this difficult?" Darcy asked, fearful, but excited in equal measure.

"Not once you've the hang of it. Dangerous, though."

"D-dangerous?"

"Oh yes. Low flying aircraft are always dangerous."

"Why fly low, then?"

"It's what Mr. Fitzgerald pays me for, at his age and all."

Lucy fiddled with the controls. Small tanks along the wingspan let out a hiss in unison, and a stream of chemicals, pesticides, almost invisible.

"You don't think he'd taught me to fly for free, did you?"

An infectious chuckle overtook the fliers.

"Happy birthday, Darcy."

"You too, Lucy."

There's No Business Like ███████

Xander Stronach

It was maybe 1962 when the G-Men came. Between Kennedy's big win in '61 and that quiet-yet-firm 6am wakeup call, I really believed we could change the world. We were living in--shit, I forget--California or Texas; somewhere hot when two men in thick black suits showed up at the door, skulking around the wee hours before the heat could flatten them. The sun will crush you whoever you are in that, she is the one true democrat.

Neither of them's very big but they make up for it in looming. My yes, those two loomed like bears, like vultures. 'Communism' is a terrible word. It's so friendly at first, then the sound underneath it hits you: communism, like rubbing together cottonballs in a darkened room. Like a lightly-loose tooth.

In maybe 1962--after Cuba and before Dallas--these two show up at our door with all the right paperwork to pull us before the House of UnAmerican Affairs. Sorry, House Committee on Un-American Activities. The agents were very picky about names; probably jealous, since they lacked their own.

Lucy was still asleep, like all reasonable people. Trust no one who is awake before the sun. Men who knock before dawn tend to find what they're looking for, whether or not it was there at all. All those little conversations at the corner store are writ down somewhere quiet and tallied up and up until you go over the "acceptable deviance threshold" and then wham, bam, you're a menace to society ma'am. They gave Lucy enough time to put on her dressing gown, then dragged her down the stairs while she swore and fought. Oh yes, two big men in black suits

56

showed those half-awake girls who's boss. I followed after them nice and quiet. No man ever put me in handcuffs without my express permission.

We came from money and we were in show business, so of course they thought we were communists. Funny thing is, there was plenty of real dirt to dig. All they had to do was follow Lucy on a Friday night and while they wouldn't find communists, they'd see no end to Un-American affairs. Apparently doing their jobs was too much work.

Instead, they hit us with the book. Books, specifically. Our library history was dragged in front of ten very serious men with very serious law degrees who stammered their way through incriminating words like "marijuana" and "female orgasm" until our lawyer was forced to stand up and make fifteen minutes' material from "FIRST AMENDMENT," which worked a charm. The Committee were suckers for the word 'America' shouted at different volumes and inflections. It let them know who their enemies were.

After that, it got nasty. They started bringing in our friends. I don't remember what they said but I remember how scared they were. They were only too happy to deflect any possible guilt onto us. Like dogs, like vultures circling in this heat. For many, the American dream died in Dallas in '63 but I know better; it was already dead and it ain't yet stopped kicking. Dead and dry under the democratic sun and staffed by vultures in big black suits and floral-print dresses.

I stopped leaving the house first. Lucy had a certain violence that kept her anchored to the world longer. She fought and swore on the stairs while I went quietly. Either way, we ended up in a cell. Welcome to America, land of the free to do as we tell you. While we were in the cell, while we were in court and while we rotted away in our house somewhere hot, I'm told the world kept turning, slow-cooking under the democratic sun. They say it's changed for the better but they'll say anything with the open sky watching them. The nice thing about -California or Texas or- someplace hot is that there's always a surplus of sun to flatten the vultures that come knocking.

The Chance Meeting at the Backstage of the Apollo Theatre, Harlem NYC

Sek Han Foo

1954

Even before she became 15, she had already known that she was adopted. Her parents - she still called them that despite her knowledge – were good people, who wanted nothing more than to keep her safe, even if it meant she would remain ignorant.

She cried for days when she found out. In time, she realized it did not matter. The important thing was the love they had for each other. Even if every time she hug or touched them, she could not help but reach for her own cleft china afterwards.

In two years' time, her parents would have left each other, and they would be taken, cruelly, by sickness and disaster. Darcy would mourn, her feelings of incompleteness never quite leaving her.

But for now, Darcy devoted herself to the piano, which her parents were happy to encourage. Darcy was learning a new sound called Bebop, something they did not understand or want to learn. Every time she played, she was in her own world.

1959

After the accident, Lucy was faced with a new reality. She had found her adoption papers in the attic, contained within a chest of secret history hidden by the recently departed.

Twin (Darcy) adpt. [Mr & Mrs W.]

The name was ambiguous, but Lucy decided immediately Darcy was her sister. Separated at birth.

As she cleaned up the house, she could not help but wonder about her sister. Was she alive? Was she well? Was she happy?

How could she find her?

When Lucy signed the papers for the sale of her parent's home, there was a space reserved for family/contact.

After some thought, she wrote "Darcy White". Then she moved to her little apartment, and got a job in the bar. In time, onstage with nothing but a cold microphone, she would get used to singing solo under the spotlight.

1965

They told her she must give a name in the event of emergencies. She tutted. "Lucy Jones," Darcy said, and pushed her way past the muscle. It was bad enough she was late - she had no patience to deal with bureaucracy that served nothing more than to remind her that she had nobody else in the world.

Why was the backstage so far away? She adjusted her step as her left heel gave way under her weight. Darcy was wondering if she should not have been too starstruck by the idea of playing in the Apollo, that she should have surveyed the place first so she would not get so ridiculously lost.

Or at least practise walking in heels. Once again they gave way, but a stagehand grabbed her just in

1965

This is crazy, thought Lucy, this is crazy and I shouldn't be here. But the other girls were too excited and happy about being in the Apollo Theatre, and there was no way Lucy could back out even if she wanted to. Time to sink or swim. Or, as Ellie always said, sing or swim.

Backstage, Ellie and Jean have already finished with their makeup and was helping Lucy with hers. Lost in her thoughts, Lucy suddenly realised that the touch up they were doing to her face was different - much much better than theirs. They hushed her when she protested. "You are the lead and you need to look unique!" they told her. She smiled, but had never felt more alone.

They got her wig on when Charlie came in to the dressing room. "Ladies!" he gave them a dazzling smile and open palms. "Absolutely gorgeous. I'm proud of you girls." He slapped Jean's bottom Jean, who feigned embarrassment and giggled. "No need to be prudish on this lovely night, my dear," he time. "Thanks," she said, and finally relented in asking for directions. He pointed at a vague location behind her, so Darcy had no choice but to retrace her steps.

She could already hear Jack yelling blue murder in her mind. He had an audience to entertain and a contract that needs to be signed, he would say, even though Darcy knew Jack smoked too little to ever get a voice that is radio-happy enough. All Darcy hoped was someone would notice the girl at the piano, which she eventually found sitting at a corner near the curtains.

She took off the covers and played a few notes. It was in tune. Bless.

Darcy was starting to play a quick chord, but she heard someone saying something about someone screaming at some girl, so she took her bag and went to the back.

She found the door, which was left slightly ajar. The backstage was teeming with people, including two girls mumbling about performing.

God, she was so late.

She was sitting down when a man pinched her bum. "Hey!" Darcy said, and slapped the phony smile off his face. It was one of those lowlife scumbags who always

said and kissed her on the cheek, then wrapped his arm around her. Jean smiled.

Lucy often wondered what the hell would possess Jean to fall in love with their manager, who Lucy figured treated his girls like hotels anyway. Then again, she herself could never settle down with some man, so who was she to judge Jean. So Lucy did what she knew best.

Smile and nod.

"Just wanna let you girls in to something..." said Charlie, "You girls are the first act of the night!"

The girls fell silent. "Oh my god I am going to die I am dead," shrieked Ellie. Jean took it by going completely numb.

"Toilet," Lucy said, and went out.

She stood in the hallway and breathed.

She needed to scream, but she had to be the calm one, or...

"There you are, bitch!" Lucy looked up. The man was marching towards her from the far end of the hall, his voice thin and weak, his exclamation notes higher than Lucy's best.

"You gonna make me go up there without music?" he was still

thought they were God's gift to women but dressed in hats three sizes too big.

"You can fuck off!" Darcy yelled at him.

The man staggered back and said he was sure she was someone he knew. Christ. Men are all the same.

She was creating a scene, and Darcy decided to just wing it without powdering her nose. Surely her talents were enough to get by all those fat cats in their zoot suits in the audience. She took her bag and went to the door.

Darcy started to leave the room.

yelling. "I could get a man to play! Fucking broads! I don't even know why I hired..."

The man was close enough to Lucy when he hesitated. He stepped back. "Shit, I thought you were someone else," he said, and walked away.

Lucy blinked, and forgot why she was in the hallway. Oh, right. Panicking bandmates. Lucy went to the door.

Lucy began to return to the room.

The twins were but babies when they were left at the orphanage, their hands holding each other's and their voices in harmony. Mother superior had, as an act of kindness, decided to put them into separate wards. She figured that it was easier for them, these two beautiful baby girls, to be adopted if they did not come in pairs. Mother superior was right, of course, for they were indeed beautiful and they were indeed taken in by two young couples, and by chance, by chance, it was on the very same day Darcy and Lucy were taken away from each other.

Mother superior was kind and great, but she was careless, and did not think of how the girls would ever know or meet each other. When she discovered her mistake, she prayed, and left it to Fate.

And Fate saw mother superior's error, and smiled.

Fate forgave mother superior, and told her, "It shall be made right."

For the girls, whose given names were Darcy Williams and Lucy Jacobs, on this night, this very night of great significance and import, hidden under the guise of the pursuit for fame and fortune, the girls, the sisters, the twins were walking towards the door, their footsteps brisk, their breaths steady, their heads held high, their arms outstretched at the same time, reaching towards the bronze doorknob of the backstage room of the Apollo, the background filled with the hushings of half-songs and the tinkling of keys and the whisper of trumpets, opening the door to the rest of their lives.

Real Lookers
Audrey Hare

We don't look it now, but we were real lookers. All the boys were after us. All the time. But we said no. Usually. Not because we wanted to, see, but because we had to. It's the curse. We have over a hundred and sixty years between us now, but we were only a couple dozen when that rotten old gypsy read our fate. It was right after Lucy kissed her first boyfriend, down on the boardwalk after work, and I was sulking jealous. We'd always done everything together, up 'til then.

I tried to get him to kiss Darcy, to keep it even, but he went right red and ran away. So, we walked out on the pier, just me and Darcy.

Lucy had bought us both a cotton candy to smooth over the kiss. I was letting it melt in my mouth, eyes closed, imagining it was my own kiss, when the scabby old claw grabbed my wrist. It was just the old lady who read fortunes, but I near jumped out of my skin. She looked at me and Darcy's palms, held them right up next to each other. We all saw, plain as day, the line run straight across mine and onto Darcy's. Then she spoke our true nature: "Your gentle touch brings death to all men." I'll be darned if Lucy's little boyfriend didn't fall off the pier and drown just two days later. We started to believe a little bit then.

Took us a while to figure out what the rules were, especially since they changed as we got older. But basically it was sex. Though Reagan went for a kiss on the cheek once, and got shot for it. Anyway, we usually said no. But not always. For a while there in L.A., our friends wondered why we only dated jerks. Then they started wondering why the jerks kept dying, not that they really minded. And it's not like we killed any of them ourselves. Well, except for Dennis. But that was self-defense. Finally, we left L.A., but it turned out there were jerks everywhere.

Kennedy was a surprise. Not that he died, of course, but that he was even interested in me at all with all the other willing, pretty girls around.

Darcy was devastated when it happened. She came home in tears saying she'd done a horrible, horrible thing.

It's true, I thought I'd ended the world! Or at least America. I did try to say no, of course, but John didn't take a no easy, and I was very tipsy.

Very tipsy, ha! Hardly captures the way we carried on in those days— little Darcy was probably half-gone to Heaven.

Maybe so, but now I feel kind of like John was a gift from the Universe. He was going to die anyway, anyone could see that. I didn't really have anything to do with it. So he's the only one I don't really feel guilty about. Well, and Dennis, I suppose. Sometimes I think Lucy got Bobby Kennedy and didn't tell anyone, just so we'd both have a Kennedy. We like to keep things even.

I did not, especially not after seeing how guilty Darcy felt right after John died, oh you should have seen her carrying on. Crying and wailing, she would have rent her clothes if she weren't so proud of them. She had a little pill box, just like Jackie used to wear. She marched us both right down to the nearest CIA office and told them everything. I hadn't done anything, but I had to go anyway, or who knew what would happen.

That's right, and that's how everything started with LBJ and how we became America's Black Widow Twins. Almost like superheroes the way they talked about us! Well, the few people who knew about us, anyway.

Lyndon tried to send us after Ho Chi Minh, first, but it was no good. The jungle was completely impassable at that point. They tried later with Jane Fonda, of course, but she didn't have much luck either. Not even with those legs of hers. She really did have spectacular legs. We did get a few Viet Kong of course, but no one really worth mentioning.

Lucy always wanted to sneak into Cambodia and go after Pol Pot, said it would make up for Kennedy.

Darcy was always too chicken, though.

We were shuffled around a bit after that. They sent us to the Middle

East, then Russia, but we really weren't so special there.

Finally they thought to send us to South America, and that's when things really got started. Chile is the most amazing place, everyone should get a chance to see it. We were officially on business, of course, but business meant acting like socialites, and we were good at that.

Former child stars, and all.

First we had General Schneider, which threw the whole army into disarray. That lead to that Marxist, Allendale, getting elected president, and so we had to go after him, too!

I don't see why we couldn't just have done him straight off in the first place.

Well, poor guy had run for president three times before and lost so I guess it's nice that he got to be president for a little while.

Before he died.

We puttered around for a while—Columbia, Nicaragua, Brazil, but eventually they brought us home. Carter wasn't as interested in our talent, we suppose. The CIA still called us every now and then for "special situations," but the calls came less and less often. They gave us a nice pension and set us out to pasture, and here we are.

The Cipher Sisters and Kid Nosferatu Dance the Bally-Kootch

Edward Morris

-for Druann Pagliasotti and Nikki Guerlain
beautiful freaks

Lucy and Darcy Schechter had two heads full of crazy, shared dreams that hot August of 1960 on the fairgrounds just outside Talequah, Oklahoma, when Kid Nosferatu slung his packsack in the rousties' tent and came to join their happy little family. He didn't stay in the rousties' tent long...

§

There were never such devoted sisters in the history of old Luigi and Paulie's travelling gilly. Both carny-bosses knew that their trade was dying, and a real act, a real McGuffin, was worth its weight in cold hard coin on the barrelhead, brother.

One of the twins had to be asleep when they did their sister-act, watching from the other's mind with both their eyes full of the Middle World. Telling her sister everything she could see. Seeing what they could See, that the Middle World showed the wakeful sister through the one who slumbered.

§

Every tin-pot sheriff tried to run their bally out of town. Sideshows weren't legal, nor natural. But the orphaned twins didn't care. They wouldn't have fit in anywhere, in a bally or a laboratory. Anyone who'd seen their act knew nothing could between them, and Lord help anyone who tried.

Well, except maybe once.

§

Words strained like honey from Time itself, raw midway honey on an elephant-ear sprinkled with powdered sugar like a bluesman's nose dusted in cocaine.

"STEP THIS WAY, FOLKS, DON'T BE SHY! THIS'N HERE AIN'T THE KOOTCH TENT, THAT'S OVER YANDER THAT WAY, NNNOT THAT THERE IS A THING WRRRRONG WITH OUR FINE COURTESAN DANCERS ETHYL AND METHYL OVER THAT WAY, BUT RRRIGHT THIS WAY, JUNIOR WILL TEAR YOUR TICKET STUB FOR YE, FOR JUST TWO BITS AND ONE HALF HOUR OF YOUR TIME YOU WILL SEE AN ACT THAT NNNO MERE HHHHHHOOTCHY-KOOTCH COULD CONTAIN..."

§

Not with that widow's peak like Bela Lugosi in the movies. Not with those spindly fingers, that looked so long it was like he had six to a hand, that he could fold and wrap and pop about, those guitar-pick-nailed hitchhiker's-thumbs. Not with the tattoos up and down his arms from cuff to shoulder. Hell fire, not with those arms, where he could pop all the joints at once and turn his hands around a full three-sixty...

§

"NOW, THE CIPHER SISTERS ARE A VERY SPECIAL SET OF TWINS FOR THE ANTONELLI & DI FILIPPO TRRRAVELLIN ROOOAD SHOW, SIDE SHOW, FREAK BALLY AAAAND RRREVUE... ANY OTHER BALLY, YOU GONNA GET YOU SOME OF THEM SIAMESE TWINS WHAT'S JOINED AT THE HEAD, OR THE

CHEST, OR... OTHER... PARTS OF WHICH DECENCY FORBIDS ME MENTION..."

§

Kid Nosferatu wasn't really a vampire like that Max Schreck in the movies, or a dope-fiend like Lugosi either. That they knew of, at first. (The rest came later.) He was an acrobat, and he was double-jointed. Big draw. The twins were twenty-one and golden-haired, golden as the Blakeian visions birthed in the hot sun and music and the hot lights of the midway when that apparition jumped from someone else's train to their own.

§

"BUT OUR OWN LUCY AND DARCY ARE EVEN MORE SPECIAL THAN THAT, KIND FRIENDS AND NEIGHBORS. THE CYPHER SISTERS ARE JOINED AT THE MIND, AND THEIR MENTALIST ACT IS NO ACT AT ALL. COME IN, COME I--- NO, ONE LINE, PLEASE. JUNIOR'LL TAKE YOUR TWO BITS, TOO..."

§

The finger of Commerce is fickle, its calliope steam-organ pipes quick to change their tune. "FOLKS," Jimbo the Barker was soon quick to belt, "BEEE-HOOLD...OUR VERY OWN VAM-PIIIRE, ALL THE WAY FROM THE OLD COUNTRY IN THE CAAAR-PATHIAN MOUNTAINS OF TRAN-SYLL-WANNIE... LOOKIT THOSE FANGS, LADIES, THAT'S ONE HHHHELLUVA HICKEY! OH...THERE HE GOES, RIGHT UP THAT WIRE. IT AIN'T LIKE IN THE MOVIES, FOLKS. THESE ONES ARE A LOOOOT HARDER TO CATCH..."

§

The name on his 4-F-rated draft card wasn't Kid Nosferatu, of course. But he looked like a kid, like one of those Beat-Mod hepcat kids from San Francisco or Manhattan or somewhere. Little tiny glasses, black wire, barely any rims. Black as the shock of hair cut on the road into a ragged sort of part, brushed back a bit. Black as the sloe-berry, black as his eyes that didn't match his alabaster skin. The alabaster skin of those strange, almost-pointed ears...

§

It could be fair to say that they both wanted him first, but not right out. Maybe the way you want to pet a wolf-dog, or a two-headed calf. On the road, any new freak in the gilly was a new toy, for a while.

Thing was, some toys were like those Russian matroshky-dolls they still kept from Mama (long after their fortuneteller Mama died on that awful midway in Yazoo City the night the big Ferris Wheel came down).

Some toys just kept opening up when you examined them, and showing more behind, beneath. Sometimes you wanted to keep playing, and sometimes you wanted to put them back.

§

It was Darcy's turn to go out. Lucy's turn to watch. Darcy wore the dress, the flesh. Lucy stayed home, the day the Kid joined them and she saw, felt, tasted...

§

O how thou art fallen from Heaven, Lucy Schechter, broken off in mid-practice by the murmuring voice of that silver-tongued waif finally daring to look Darcy in the eyes and mutter, "No, that part just looks normal. Little bit banged up, and there's Bond-O on some parts, got it running with a coathanger and part of a... WELL you don't mess around, do you? Please don't squeeze so hard, it's been a while since.---"

§

On the other side of the connection, the April witch squirms on the mattress she designed for her own dreamings, when they practiced the act, when she practiced with her sister and volunteered to fold her hands over her pale bosom like Snow White and go down to Dream, make the diamond-shape in her mind (like that old wet-brained Geek did in snake's blood at that other carny they saw in Texas that time) and open up her inner eye, and see...

§

Oh God, See...the way Darcy thumb-locked both Kid Nosferatu's wickedly strong hands, the way the rousties taught her to, and pinned them behind his head, hooked his ankles and nearly beat him to the floor. The way she straddled him and fucked him like she had the cock, and made the odd creature shriek like a banshee until she decided to turn him loose...

Lucy could only marvel at the forthrightness of her dear sister. It had been a long time on the road. But soon enough, none of them needed words.

Most especially not her. And when Lucy woke, trembling, the road looked less gray and dusty, the fairgrounds full of the clear light she only saw when she made the diamond in her mind. Everything shone. Everything...

Asymmetry
Amanda Gowin

By sixteen she could no longer remember a time when she knew which was her mother. Neither answered to Mother; neither answered much of anything she said.

Her first memories were of the picture books in her blue bedroom.

The shelves were lined with toys – two music boxes with broken gears, their identical ballerinas frozen in identical icy poses. A wind-up seesaw missing its key, stopped even, balanced, a faceless girl at each end. Porcelain dolls, temples touching, eyes shining and secretive. But in the books there were drawings of men and women, a child between them. Her four-year-old self traced the men's faces with curious hands. She had never seen a Him. The princesses in the towers waited for Him, the devil that spun straw into gold was Him, the man in the sky that burned the bad people was Him.

Did you make me? she'd asked.

The twins' eyes met.

Not together, one answered.

But you're ours all the same, said the other.

In one of them she had grown and swam, a single mermaid in a single bowl, but she could not guess which.

At six she spent most of her time on the porch swing, the wind chime's rusty metal efforts the closest thing to a lullaby she heard. It clinked and shimmered desperately, aching to soothe her as she lay with a teddy bear under each arm and thanked it quietly. There was no other half of her, therefore she was alone. From the vegetable garden came laughter and gibberish, a language not her own and a language they did not teach her. They taught her the 'outside language' and how to read from sepia books, flanking her at the kitchen table.

I know there are schools, she'd said.

Out there is not for us, one answered.

Out there they're not like us, said the other.

But I am not like you, she didn't say. I am not part of this Us.

She realized they hadn't meant her inclusion, anyway. There was no word for Mother in their language, she supposed, but hundreds and hundreds for We.

So the wind chime was her mother's voice, the moon her mother's face. The wind chime asked in broken notes, the moon tilted its head, waiting for answers. Nighttime conversations of whispers floated in and out her open window while her chin rested on the sill.

At the edge of the driveway she stood for hours, eight years old, to study the outside faces glimpsed in occasional cars. She searched for doubles through the gravel dust, and her surprise was never exhausted by the absence. I am one of Them, she thought. Pairs of yellow butterflies danced in rising circles in the light fluttering between the branches of the big tree, taunting her. Beneath it, all things were halves of a whole.

Where is mine? she'd asked.

In the mirror, said one.

In the mirror you're never incomplete, said the other.

Their eyes locked in pity at the loneliness they could not understand.

Twelve and wild with emptiness, she'd run on bare feet and brown legs through the fields, forever and ever, tall grass whipping her skin, sunshine filling her lungs -- and heart. It swelled and broke with every breath, cracking over and over with the double beat in her chest. In a clearing squatted a wide and gnarled stump, day after day she found herself upon it, reaching for the sky, spreading her fingers with face upturned, becoming the other half of this tree. Sun between her fingers, sun leaking from her eyes, she dreamed of the roots spread beneath the ground in a mirror image.

She ran out of questions, forgot her voice. She was the animal that roamed the grounds of their castle – a skittish deer they watched with curious eyes, but never extended a hand to tame.

The mirror in her room was the only mirror in the house, and she saw it for what it was: a surrogate, a stand-in, the only thing they knew to give her to help bear what she lacked. She smashed it into hundreds of miniature sixteen year old girls – the temptation to count them seized her, sure the number of shards would be even, casting her out once again.

The stairs moaned at the twins' rapid ascent, two faces, two pairs of wide dark eyes in her doorway.

You've killed her, said one.

What will you do now? asked the other.

I could leave, she said.

Silence clung to the corners of the room.

It's time to let her go, said one.

And the other said nothing. A pale arm extended, and with a ragged fingernail scratched at the skull of one of the dolls on the seesaw, breaking the balance, revealing a sliver of blond beneath the hand-painted hair.

That night in the dark house, her window stood open and the moonlight tossed a gossamer rectangle across the shards of glass. She pushed the pieces carefully around. Outside, the wind chime shivered silver notes, silver tears, and downstairs one twin cried.

Darcy and Lucy Among the Flowers

Alexander Davis

Darcy brought home roadkill on Friday, to do a favor for Mr. and Mrs. Borlin. Lucy said she thought probably it had been an opossum, and Darcy told her, "Possum."

Lucy put it on one of the floral plates they'd inherited from their mother. "It was Opossum, I always thought."

Darcy said, "Well that's how it's spelled."

Lucy said, "Right, I said that."

Darcy said, "The O is silent, Loo, you're being silly."

Lucy said, "Oh."

They brought the roadkill to the kitchen, and Lucy put it on the table near the carrot plant. The carrot plant had not flowered, but they didn't mind. People who came over for readings or other such things (mostly acquaintances, friends of friends, or folks who had heard of them from word-of mouth; the weird sisters did not advertise) remarked, sometimes, about what a lovely house they had, but don't you ladies have any kind of flowers somewhere? Lucy once suggested they plant a petunia or something. To be more like the nice little old ladies they were expected to be. Darcy refused.

Darcy had never cared for flowers after 1964, the year their father vanished and the frilly things engaged their mourning mother in a long and decaying infatuation. Buttercups and Forsythia crept out of her pockets and weaved their way into her hair. Eventually they escaped into the picture frames once occupied by the faces of her children, and their mother no longer recognized them when they visited to tidy up. The flowers squeezed themselves between the pages of her books, and she could no longer read. Wiry doily forms of roses and orchids stretched across everything she owned, engraving themselves where they couldn't be painted. They snaked across her bed, and trapped her inside. Right before she was put in the ground the flowers crowded the coffin so closely the twins couldn't see her body. Darcy entertained the theory that some scheming clematis had smuggled her in her sleep. So they hid the flowery plates, and only took them out again when they had something nasty to put on them. They very often did.

Darcy went to get her glasses, and the Book. Lucy poked the roadkill. There were still tufts of fur there, and maybe a foot, to indicate the brown-and-red soup had once been a living thing. She stroked what may have once been its head, felt the liquidated insides shift and give behind the ruined skin. Darcy reentered the room, her large Book in tow, and told her, "Don't touch it. We've no idea where it's been."

Lucy said, "We have, it's been across the road."

"Well," said Darcy. "One, Lucy, soft brained sister mine, it's been halfway across the road, and two you can get all sorts of horrifying flesh-eating diseases from small animals like this. Scoot over."

Lucy scooted over, and Darcy sat down next to her, dropping the Book on the table. It landed with a jarring thump and flopped open like the clumsy first wingbeat of a startled crow. As she leafed through the pages the twins caught snatches of pentacles and withered things in jars and vaporous demons. Fanciful little horrors the young occultists loved sketching in everything they wrote.

Lucy had been apprehensive when Darcy brought home the Book. They had always done readings the way their father Garmin (The Great Garmin, his stage name was) had taught them, before he did that disappearing-in-a-mirror trick of his and never showed up again. With a palm and, if they felt fancy, a crystal. Nice and traditional. Lucy had a lovely headscarf to wear for the occasion. The Book was in her estimation very near a Tome, and she had no truck with any sort of Tome. Darcy reassured her that this was mostly just a sort of cookbook. Like the cookbook she had gotten her blintz recipe from, and didn't Lucy love her blintzes?

Darcy was not looking for blintzes in the Book. She was searching (and it was somewhere in the back, she recalled) for a conjuration she'd first done on Mr. Morey's cat, Scouter, at his request. It hadn't been permanent, of course, but at least the poor old fellow got some time to say goodbye. She'd used it next on Mr. Morey for Mrs. Morey, who had requested the same opportunity after her husband's last stroke. It was a good thing they didn't have any children, because they had just about used up their free favors from the twins, as far as Darcy saw it. When she found the diagram she sent Lucy upstairs to go get her Pink Penny lipstick, which would do nicely for the circle. She moved the table to one side of the kitchen and piled the chairs up next to it. Lucy arrived with the lipstick, frowning. "Lift the chairs next time, Darcy, or you'll make scuffs."

Darcy took the lipstick from her and began the arduous process of bending down to all fours. "I did lift them."

"You did not," Lucy told her. "I heard them scraping across the floor from upstairs."

"You're deaf as a post, you rickety hag," Darcy said. "And anyway," she told the grout, "you try lifting one of those without throwing something out."

"I like our linoleum spotless, thank you," Lucy said.

Darcy pulled the top of the lipstick off with her teeth. "Then you're going to get very cross with me in a second."

It was a well-done circle. Lucy admitted as much after she had stopped yelling and calmed down a little. The sigils along its circumference were set down with the smooth hand of a calligraphist and the critical eye of an expert. Darcy rebutted with the frank insinuation that her bones shook loud enough to be audible and she had so many cataracts you could probably peel them off with a paring knife, but Lucy knew she was glowing on the inside. She was fiercely proud of her skill at witchcraft.

They took up the floral plate and gingerly placed it in the middle of the circle, where the arcing strokes of the runes converged and intertwined into a leering death's head. Lucy had thought they might try making it look like a cat skull for Scouter, back when they were unfamiliar with this little charm, but after deliberation they had agreed it probably wouldn't be a good idea. Darcy rose with difficulty from the middle of the circle, careful not to smudge anything, and stood next to Lucy, surveying her work.

"Well, go ahead, Loo," she said. "You have the better voice for this sort of thing."

Lucy - who had been the singer of the pair back in the heady performative days - cleared her throat, coughed once, and raised her arms above her head, her bangles jingling. "I really should have my headscarf for this," she said. "Ahem. Rise, disenfranchised spirit long threaded through the veil, long submerged! Rise! By the pact Adam made with crowned Death as it pursued him from his arboreal seat, rise! Rise up!"

The floral plate vibrated, then rattled, then jumped violently up and down on the floor. The ruin of gore and fur upon it writhed, and the twins heard the snapping of its crushed bones as it tried to crawl upright. A rasping, clattering voice rose from the roadkill, not tonally dissimilar to the crashing plate. It said:

SHIT. SHIT AUGHSHIT CAR AUGH. IT WAS A CAR. NOOO. SHIT, CAR. MY BRAIN IS DASHED ON THE ASPHALT: I AM A GREASE STAIN. SHIT.

"Tell it to watch its language," said Darcy. "And ask about the Borlin boy."

"Watch your language in our home, Mr. Opossum," said Lucy. "Uh, Possum. I charge you. With the fell knowledge of your Cimmerian home: When shall be the death of Terry Borlin, age 11?"

SHIT. SHIT ON YOUR HOME, WITCHWOMAN. AUGHH, NO. CAR.

The mass on the plate twitched violently. Its congealed blood made sticky tearing noises against the china.

CRUSH METAL SQUELCH MUTILATE TEAR; DESPAIR. TERRY BORLIN DIES IN THREE DAYS' TIME. HE WILL NEVER LEAVE THE HOSPITAL AND HE WILL DIE IN THE HOSPITAL. SHITCAR. HE WILL JOIN ME IN THE SUNLESS LAND SO AS YOU ALL WILL JOIN

ME SOON. NO MATTER HOW FAST YOU MAKE YOUR KILLING CARS GO YOU WILL NOT OUTRUN DEATH. CAR.

"Oh, dear," said Darcy. "That's that, then. I suppose we should call Mrs. Borlin. Poor dear. You can tell the rodent to leave, Lucy. Thank you, Possum."

YOUR FATHER IS DEAD. HE PASSED INTO THE MIRROR AND THE THING ON THE OTHER SIDE ATE HIM. HE DIED AND YOU'LL DIE. YOUR MAGIC WILL NOT SAVE YOU. CARCARCAR AUGH. THE FLOWERS WIN. THEY'LL GROW OVER YOU.

"Yes, well, he'd be dead by now one way or the other." Darcy started putting the chairs back.

Lucy started to lower her arms and then hesitated. "Before you leave, I charge you to divine one more death: When shall be my--" but Darcy, with the speed of a woman fifty years her junior, leaped behind her sister and pinned her arms to her sides. The plate fell still.

"That sort of masturbatory question is poor form for a self-respecting witch," said Darcy, gently relinquishing her talon grip on Lucy's forearm. "And besides: don't you appreciate death's little mysteries?"

Lucky
DB Cox

—For my Grandfather

On Sunday mornings we'd march to the church. The preacher would tell us how Jesus loved the little children and we'd sing this tune:

"Jesus loves the little children

All the children of the world

Red and yellow, black and white

They are precious in his sight…"

Sometimes, after church, our grandfather would drive down in his Hudson and take us for a ride. It was the only time we got to go off the grounds of the Kelly Ridge Home for Girls. Darcy and I would take turns sitting next to Grandfather. We'd listen to songs on the radio and I'd admire that old fedora he always wore. I wondered why there were no songs about my grandfather.

My name is Lucy, but my twin sister, Darcy, has always called me Lucky. When she was little she had trouble saying my name. It always came out sounding like Lucky. My parents thought it was cute, so the nickname stuck.

Kelly Ridge Home for Girls is a place for young girls who have been abandoned, abused, or neglected. It used to be called Kelly Ridge Orphanage, but I guess the word "Home" is a kinder-sounding word.

Here, you grow up crowded—crowded into the same bedroom—crowded into the same bathroom—crowded into the same dining room. You even end up wearing other kids' clothes, or you see one of your favorite old shirts, years after you last wore it, on some other girl's back.

We came here in 1945 when we were six years old. For the last seven years, we have lived in this strange world of cast-off children—kids who no longer believe in humans and don't have a reason to believe in Gods. We work. We play. We stay busy to forget. We no longer question or expect. We have learned that silence is a response.

When we were younger, Darcy and I would make wild plans to run away—slip into the night and head for home. We would pretend we were serious, but we knew it was just a game. There was nothing to run toward except an empty box of bad times.

> Our mother: Voices in her head—drip, drip, dripping
> like a broken faucet—louder and louder—until she ran for
> the door like the house was on fire.

> Our father: Sleeping alone behind closed doors—lost
> in drunken dreams—an imagined world where everything
> was still in its place.

> I can barely remember their faces—no photo smiles
> frozen in place—the sound of voices fading to gray.

Mother never looked back, but I've never blamed her. Back then her fear was the same as mine. I hope she was able to turn herself into something brand new and beautiful again.

§

Three months after our mother left, Darcy and I, both five years old, found our father in his bedroom swinging from an electric cord—face as black as the socks on his feet.

I covered Darcy's eyes with my hands, led her out of the room, and closed the door. She didn't say a word. She just stood there with her back against the living room wall. When I asked her if she was okay, she whispered, "Please don't talk."

I called my grandfather. I held Darcy until he came with the police and an ambulance.

Neither of us cried at the funeral. We just sat with grandfather staring straight ahead while a stranger said nice things about our father.

§

Last night Darcy woke up screaming. She was yelling, "Please daddy. Please daddy. I promise. I'll do anything you say."

When Darcy wakes up afraid she has to know where she is. She needs to see right away. So, when I heard her cry out, I hurried to turn on the lights.

When I got to her bed, she had her hands in front of her face. I hugged her close and watched her hands shake. When she calmed down, she rested her cheek against my arm, looked up at me and said, "Lucky, tell me a story. Tell me about the house where we will live."

"Close your eyes and I'll tell you the story."

Someday, when we leave this place, we're going to find a house—a perfect house where we will live forever. It will be a big, white house in an open space—a place with wide windows that are easy to see through—windows with clear panes where no secrets can hide. The front door will always be unlocked and it will open onto a clean street that leads to a park where we can take our Golden Retriever to play in the evening.

And on weekends, we'll jump in our yellow convertible and drive it too fast down Highway One, along the Pacific Coast Highway, our hair whipping in the wind as it pours through the open top. We'll ride through the salt-smelling air until we're sunburned and tired of moving. Then we'll find a place to stop—a place where the music is loud, and they serve shrimp and crabmeat and ice-cold watermelon. After eating too much, we'll drink red wine and dance with handsome men until the sun comes up…

I watch for most of the night while she sleeps, warm and quiet, in my arms.

§

"Starlings are mean, ugly birds," said Darcy, "and they can't sing like a redbird."

We are standing off to the side of the road watching a bird that's been hit by a car. It's on its back, squawking, in the middle of the street. One wing is broken and the other is flapping like crazy in a hopeless struggle to fly. The injured starling can only spin round and round in a small circle.

The bird, finally exhausted from his effort, stops fighting and becomes still. His head is pushed to one side against the pavement. One dark, terrified eye is staring up at me. He seems to be waiting for someone to do something.

I strip off my T-shirt and walk into the street. I throw the shirt over the bird, cup my hands around the fluttering lump, and scoop it off the pavement.

I carry the bird across the yard and back to our cottage. I walk upstairs to the bathroom and turn on the water in the bathtub. Holding the shirt with my left hand, I push the rubber stopper into drain. When the tub is full, I turn off the water, kneel down, and push the shirt all the way under.

The starling is still trying to fly, beating its one good wing against the cloth. When the bird stops moving, I lift the shirt out of the water, walk downstairs, and out the backdoor.

There's a metal trashcan sitting next to the storage shed. I walk over, open the shirt, and let the dead bird fall into the can. The body gives a small quiver—one last denial of the facts. I drop my shirt over the ugly bird.

Like always, Darcy just follows along—asking nothing—saying nothing. She never questions anything I do.

Sometimes, the older girls ask, "What's wrong with her? Why is she always following you around?"

But they really don't want to know.

§

The first time I saw my father hit my mother we were all sitting at the kitchen table having dinner. They were arguing. I don't remember what it was about. I guess it must have been pretty important. As they shouted back and forth, they started to seem like strangers to me.

When it happened, it was so fast, I'm not sure if I actually saw it. There was the sudden crack of my father's hand against my mother's face, and I found myself standing up—hands flat on the tabletop. Darcy didn't move. She just sat there with her head down—eyes locked on her plate.

Then I saw my father's face change as he looked first at me, then at Darcy, then back at me. He looked confused and scared. His eyes seemed to be asking for something. What? At the time, I didn't know. But now, I believe my father was asking to be rescued. He wanted someone to save him. He wanted me to save him.

But how can you reach inside the walls of a person's soul?

Our mother sat at the table, blood coming from the corner of her mouth, wiping at her eyes with a wrinkled napkin. She had already started to disappear.

§

Our grandfather died this past July, of Alzheimer's Disease. He spent his last years in the County Home. One time the preacher took us to visit him, but he didn't know who we were. He just sat there with the others in the "day room" staring at the screen of a silent television.

They all looked like they were

expecting something to change.

On the way back to the campus Darcy and I sat in the backseat of the preacher's car holding hands and crying silently for our grandfather. We never went to see him again. And when he passed away, we didn't go to the funeral.

By then, he had been gone for a long time.

We loved our grandfather and he loved us. He was our last connection to the outside world.

§

In a few years, my sister and I will have to leave this place—this tiny world where all of the decisions are made for us. Orphanages only protect children until they turn eighteen. They call it "aging out." If you haven't been adopted by then, ready or not, you have to hit the streets—no place to call home—nothing and nobody to fall back on.

Lately I've started to worry about what this means for Darcy and me. I know that whatever we do we'll have to do it together. As long as I have Darcy to love and protect, I am alive.

§

Downstairs in our cottage there's an old piano that nobody plays. Sometimes late at night when I'm feeling afraid about the future I slip down to the living room. I sit in front of the long row of keys and bend my right ear toward the strings. I hit the lowest note and push the pedal to the floor. Then I close my eyes and listen as the note rings out its one-tone song and I think about that tune we used to sing in Sunday School: "Jesus loves the little children…"

I wonder if there really is a Jesus. And if he loves us now, will he still love us when we "age out?" When we're no longer children, will we still be precious in his sight?

1951
Matt McGee

I think I can fill in a few things about the lives of the Cipher sisters, though really I don't feel it's much of anyone's business and that it won't lead to the eventual solving of their mysterious deaths. Frankly, what I have to offer you is merely an anecdote of two young girls I once knew, and maybe you'll see something in it that will help you glue the pieces together, much like the beautiful vase Lucy once smashed in our house, a relic my father had brought back from the Marshall Islands. But will it help you out? I make no promises.

You see, this is what old men do. We sit around and tell you stories about bullshit that happened a really, really long time ago whether or not it has any impact on you or not. We think it's relevant to your current life–we certainly like to think it is–because otherwise what have our lives added up to if we can't pass on to the next generation (and all the others, for that matter) the experiences we've had? I thank you, actually, for giving me a chance to spill this particular little anecdote.

The sisters were friends of mine. Well, Darcy was, since we just hit it off one day when I was playing in a stickball game here on Hedgeford Ave., the street I was born and raised on. I believe Lucy, Darcy and her folks (did they have folks? You know, I'm really not sure, cause now that I think about it I never saw them). Well, I guess Lucy and a couple of her girlfriends found out that a lot of boys were hanging out in one spot, and since a couple of the older ones wanted to go see what was happening, maybe stare at Bobby Kilcullen with his shirt off (that guy got all the girls man, he taught me about things I still don't think are human). Bear in mind I was only eleven at the time, which would make Lucy and Darcy a year older. To me girls weren't much to shake a stick at, but little did I know. Apparently they already had designs in their heads. While we were busy playing ball and making broke-down wagons into downhill racers, the girls were already plotting things without us boys having a single clue. But I'm off on a tangent. That's what old guys do.

So we're in the middle of this hot stickball game in the middle of Hedgeford when up walks Lucy and a couple of girls. I didn't know her at the time but she was walking next to Katie Lee Robb, who was hot stuff in our grade. I was a pretty smart kid, and Katie was definitely smarter than me. Or is it "I?" Either way she was smarter. Or she applied herself better. Whichever it was, there was a definite tension between us that lasted for years. We were competitive bookworms, nowadays someone you'd call a nerd. She was pretty to boot, and so the other girls either gravitated to her or hated her, but mostly they drew right to her. Just like the rest of us boys. Yep, I hung my tongue out for Katie like a dog on a hot day.

So here she comes down the street, Lucy Miller in tow, and another girl next to Lucy who I would later find out was her sister, Darcy. The twins looked alike but, if you'd been around them long enough you could tell who was you, you know? You got to know the nuances of their voices, choices of colors and clothes, the way they stepped along and held themselves. Little things. Well, Lucy and I hit it off right away, kind of. Being as we were only kids at the time there's only so much to 'hitting it off', and now that I think back on it, I think Katie must have put a bug in her ear, you know, about our being competitive with one another in school. It's just like girls to do that – the girls I've known, anyway, you know. One gets to liking a boy, and next thing you know the friend has got designs on the guy herself. Turns into this whole Archie comic kind of competition, this rivalry. Silliness if you ask me. But either way, there they were.

Katie introduced me to Lucy, who then introduced me to her sister, Darcy. That was the other girl in the pack that day, Darcy. Well Lucy says something funny, something about "Hey, I saw you up to bat last inning. I hope you do better on your next chemistry test than you do out there on the field." The girls all had a laugh at my expense, and it burned me up of course, Katie and I being rivals and all. I suspect Katie put her up to it, but I never found out that part of the story.

I said, "Oh yeah? Maybe you should come up to bat here and take my spot, you're so good at it." I thought I had her dead to rights on that one. No girl who's dressed as pretty as she is, hanging around a fashion plate like Katie Lee Cobb is going to scuff up her nice shoes and risk soiling her dress playing in any ol' stickball game.

Well, she showed me. The next time it was my turn to bat, I grabbed the stick from Stevie Polansky and started toward the batter's box. I'm maybe, what, four steps toward the plate when suddenly up from behind me like a stealth jet comes Lucy. She swipes the stick out of my hand and steps ahead of me. I'll never forget the little shove in the chest she gave me. It was the first time I'd ever really been in contact with a girl. Kind of a strange way to get started if you ask me.

"Step back, bookworm," she said. "The babe is up to bat now."

The girls all laughed and, I gotta admit, a few of the boys thought it was funny too. No one had heard a girl be so brazen as to call herself a babe before. Usually that was reserved to us guys and the nasty little discussions we'd have in our various hangouts around the neighborhood– the empty lots and in the backseat of the abandoned Model H on the Polansky's property. For all I know she was likening herself to Babe Ruth. Who knows.

She stepped up to the plate and got in the crouch. The catcher looked her over, looked at me, then shrugged. The ump was all set to call 'play ball' but Jimmy Stubbs, the pitcher, was going to have something to say about it.

"Wait just a minute," he yells, "I ain't pitchin' to no goddamn girl! Hey why don't you go back to reading Little Women, huh? Leave the boys to play their boy game."

Well I figure that had done it right there, she'd break down crying on the spot, drop the stick and run home. I was just taking a step toward home plate when she took another practice swing.

"What's the matter, afraid of being embarrassed by a girl?" Lucy was a pisspot this way. She really knew how to get to a guy's feathers in a bunch.

"Aw go on," Jimmy waved his glove. It was a second-hand model his uncle had given him. He'd told us all that his uncle had played for the

Senators and this had been his uncle's glove. Frankly none of us believed him, but who were we to question the kid with the rubber arm who didn't mind pitching for three hours in the street? Besides, he always came with the ball (he said his uncle gave him those too, and one of them did say 'National League' on it, so maybe there was something to it after all).

"Go on," he said again, "beat it. I ain't pitching to no sissy girl."

This time, Katie spoke up. "Aw go on Whitey Ford, pitch to her!"

Now bear in mind, it wasn't just me that was sweet on Katie Lee Cobb. But if I had a crush on her, Jimmy was a full-blown, head-over-heels idiot for Katie. He tried to argue with her, but Katie just kept throwing it back at him. Katie was his weakness, so finally he waved her off and said "Fine, just don't go crying to your daddy when you skin your knee."

The first pitch he threw her was a patent Jimmy Stubbs fastball. Now, most of us skilled guys who played regularly, if not every day, hoped and dreamed of coming close to taking a half-assed swing at one of Jimmy's heaters. It was real magic what he had, or at least a lot of practice. Maybe he was just showing off for Katie. Either way, the ball flew past Lucy and into the catchers mitt and I'm not sure, but I think Lucy's mouth was still open, I think she was ready to babble something else out when the pitch flew past.

"Hey, not fair! I wasn't ready!" she shouted. The catcher threw the ball back to Jimmy.

"Well girlie, ready or not, here it comes again!"

Jimmy let loose with heater number two, a real smoker, and it came in at the catcher's mitt in record time. Lucy squinted her face, I can still see her doing it, and swung the stick with all her might, but the ball had already passed her.

"Strike two!" the umpire called. The guys on the infield cheered. Katie and Darcy shouted words of encouragement from the sidewalk. I just stood there beside the girls, trying not to look like a girl-sympathizer but, at the same time, no one noticed just how I was inching closer, slowly closer to Katie's side. I could almost smell her and had forgotten my own lost at-bat when Jimmy let tear with his third pitch.

Anyone who was around that day will tell you what happened next. The ball flew right past Lucy like the first two, she took the best swing she could muster, and the ump called her out. The guys cheered like we'd just beat the Germans all over again, and the girls started arguing with the umpire about the pitch being outside, or too low, or whatever they thought would work to get Lucy another swing. But when you're out you're out. At the moment that the next incident happened, I recall it was Katie, Lucy, the catcher and the ump in a cluster screaming at each other.

Jimmy had just started moving toward the group of them and was calling something out that filled his ears, which kept him from hearing the screech of tires down at the end of the block. The rest of us facing that direction saw and heard it, but Jimmy had his back to the Packard as it careened down Hedgeford, full speed into our outfield. Other kids shouted and scattered, seeing it coming from a distance. Jimmy, still arguing about girls playing ball, didn't have a clue.

Katie, who'd been arguing good-naturedly with the ump, saw the car coming and saw that Jimmy didn't. The thing I think we all remember best, and I know I certainly do, is that Katie took off, full sprint like Superman, head-on toward Jimmy and the car. The rest of us scattered for cover, but Katie just ran right into it. We coulda' used her in the war.

When that Packard blew into our playing field, Katie hit Jimmy with the full weight of her body and knocked him down with a tackle that would've made Knute Rockne proud as all hell. They landed on the pavement, both of them, she on top, and rolled part way under my Dad's '49 Crown Vic. When the Packard blew past us, and I can still smell the exhaust in my nose, I think it was a miracle that it hadn't smeared at least one of us or bounced us up into the air and onto the sidewalk. One of us could have easily been killed, and more than anyone – it should have been Jimmy.

As everyone started to get their bearings, we looked up and toward the end of the street for a cop on a motorbike or someone else to come chasing after the Packard, but apparently we'd been listening to too many episodes of Gangbusters because it never happened. It was just some older kids, just having scraped together enough for a second-hand junker taking it out for a drag. We picked up our gloves, our friends, and thought about putting everyone back together to finish the game but we knew better than to tempt fate. We all kind of looked at each other with this 'What do we do now?' kind of stare.

That's when we saw Katie and Jimmy, still under my Dad's Ford. Whatever it was they were doing down there I don't know, but we all kind of looked at each other awkwardly, not knowing what to say. The girls, it seemed to be Lucy most of all, were all smiling from ear to ear.

You could hear the two of them talking quietly to each other, and that's about the moment I knew. I knew, from that moment on, I would never have a chance of dating Katie Lee Cobb. Jimmy had a hold on her, literally, and never let her go. After he did a stint in the Army, which you just plain did in those days (and hey, Elvis did it, so how uncool could it be?), he and Katie married.

But that, of course, isn't all there is to the incident. As mothers do, a few of them had been standing nearby or on stoops and came running to sort out the whole melee. When they saw Jimmy and Katie tucked under the Ford, they dragged them both up and, it was my mom I'm proud to say, who insisted that Jimmy come inside the house and get cleaned up. He was bleeding from his arms and elbows, had a cut on his ear and a scrape on his head and cheek from where Katie had levelled him into the asphalt. The girls all ran up to the scene. They'd read Florence Nightingale and wanted to help. Mom and Katie led Jimmy up the stairs to our front room, with Lucy and Darcy in tow to attend to his wounds.

When I looked back at the street, the guys were all standing with hands on their hips. No one really wanted to play ball anymore. A few of them were cutting toward home. A couple others were being led off by their mothers, who cursed the older kids for nearly killing their offspring and muttered about "getting a decent lot for you boys and girls to play your little games in."

Back in my house it was Operation Hospital. You'd have thought Jimmy had been shot in the damn war or something the way the girls were fussing over him. Mom supplied the iodine and went to the wall to make a call to Mrs. Stubbs. "He's OK, but you should probably come right over and get him," she said. Jimmy told my mom how embarrassing this was, but Katie dabbing a little iodine gently to his cheek seemed to shut him up. I think he even smiled.

Lucy said "I'm real sorry I made you pitch to me, Jimmy. I just wanted you to let us girls have a chance, that's all."

"Aw," he waved his hand. "Don't worry about it. You didn't know what you were getting into. It's a boys game for corn's sake." At that Katie pressed the cotton a little harder into his cheek and he let out a hiss. "Hey, easy there," he said. She smiled at him, and he reluctantly smiled back. Lucy said "Don't hurt him too bad Katie. He's just a boy, after all."

Everyone laughed at this, and I don't remember what was said or done for the next few minutes, but I do remember this next part clear as day. Because you don't forget the moment the first time you notice someone you've never noticed before.

I walked into the living room, the one where my Dad would sit and grade his school papers, shake his head and mumble to my Mom about how hard he worked and yet the kids today weren't getting a decent education at home. Only recently had he allowed us to get a radio, and television was damn near in every household around us yet we wouldn't have one until after I left for college.

When I walked into the living room, I begin to hear voices. I'd forgotten what time it was, and for that matter what day, but someone hadn't. There, sat right down in the middle of the living room with the radio turned on was Darcy. She had the station tuned into my favorite radio show, The Great Gildersleeve. Looking back on those old shows they do seem kind of hokey and simplistic, but I liked them. We all did. But I especially liked Gildersleeve, always being a blow-hard and ticking off the local judge or hanging out with Old Mr. Peavey in the drugstore. But most of all, Gildy had a way of charming the girls. It just seemed completely natural to him. Little did I know it was writers of the show who were helping Gildy overcome his shyness.

Well, it would be Darcy who helped me overcome my shyness that day. When I saw her sitting there, I said "Hey, what are you doing? That's our radio. You can't just come in and make yourself at home."

Instead of arguing, or making a fuss like her sister Lucy had, Darcy just reached over and patted the carpet beside her with her hand, telling me to have a seat. Well, to this day, no matter what kind of 'Ick, it's a girl' kind of instinct I was still clinging to, sure enough, I went over and sat down next to Darcy and listened to what turned out to be our favorite radio show. You know how some people have 'our song?' Well, we had the voice of the Gildersleeve. In fact, just because I'm talking about it, I'll tell you that our first real date, when I had a car and a little part time job–the first time I took Darcy out for real was when my Dad, through his work, had got a couple tickets to a live broadcast of The Great Gildersleeve.' Darcy and I went, totally enthralled to be seeing the fat man in person. December 14, 1956. The show was just about off the air by then. We made it in just under the wire.

But that day, and that's why I've been telling you this whole damn story, is because of what happened right in the middle of the show. There we sat, Darcy and I, side by side, listening to the show, touching hands, when out of another room comes this loud crash. It was the kind of noise you associate with someone being injured, having fallen over and toppled whatever was in their way. Suddenly we were hearing the women's voices and the mutter of scrambling bodies through the house to see what was going on. Darcy and I, well, we just sat and kept listening to our program. Whatever was going on, someone would handle it. We were busy. We were falling in love.

And as it turns out, that was the problem. Apparently Lucy, having seen Katie and Jimmy fawning over each other in the kitchen, tried to get out of their hair and let their romance bud (despite the fact that my mother was still in the room, tending to his cuts and, as she always did in a time of crisis, making sandwiches). On her way out of the front room, Lucy stumbled upon us, without our knowing, and had seen us holding hands. Suddenly, to her young mind, everyone had been coupled up in the blink of an eye. For Christ's sake, in her mind even my mother had my father on his way home soon enough.

Lucy, feeling like everyone's third wheel, made for the front door. And on her way out, being overwrought with emotion or whatever was stuck in her craw, she bumped the entryway table with her hip, knocking down that vase my Dad had shipped home during his tour in the Marshall Islands. It shattered into a million pieces, it was completely unfixable, and only added embarrassment to Lucy's already overwhelming feeling of inadequacy as a woman. She swore to fix it, or replace it, or find another one, but this was long before Ebay and besides, her family didn't have any money. It never got fixed or replaced, just swept up and dumped into the waste can. Actually, I don't think mother ever told my father about it, and for all I know he never noticed. The only one who really remembered it was Lucy, as Darcy told me that over the years Lucy searched far and wide for another one like it.

We never married but we stayed in contact, Darcy and I, but Lucy, I think that day in the ballgame was her shining moment. Of course, that's just one old man's opinion. For all I know she became ambassador to Japan and lived a full life. But I don't really know. But I still think about both of them–especially when I tune in my local radio station on Sunday nights and hear that familiar booming voice come flying back to me from the past on Stan Freeburg's 'When Radio Was' show. I think to call Darcy, but last I heard we don't live anywhere near each other. And I think to call Lucy, especially when life gets hard and seems to go to a million pieces, because there are days that, if I had a chance, I'd step back and ask if she wants to pinch hit for me.

The Sister is The Sister

edward j rathke

It was a map and it was her face. Canyons dug by time, ridges and precipices, memories of long gone days. Folds and creases made by unseen hands over a lifetime, their lifetime.

Time.

Time carved and wore down their faces, stretched their skin, stole their lustre. All of this taken by Time. Time who hid it. Hid it where they always looked deepest. Hid it where it would never be lost to love. Time stole all that they were, all their beauty and brilliance, and stored it in the eyes of the other. The eyes. Maps to their own shared and separate pasts. Every thought, dream, and prophecy stared back at them even as they projected new ones into those chasms.

You are my sister.

I am your sister.

You are me.

No, but we are one.

What will happen when I die?

I will come too, the sister said to her sister. Lie down now, dear. Rest. Sleep well and easy. You and I may die, but we will live forever in the dreams we share.

The sister tucked in her sister and shuffled on stiff and bony legs to the window where she watched for signs of the star.

§

The sister traced the smooth jaw of her reflection who kissed her. The sister and the sister undid the hair tied in buns, removed the dresses, and washed the makeup away. The sister and the sister stared at the mirror and then at one another. Hands to hands and breasts to breasts and forehead to forehead, they pushed away, clasping hands, bracing feet to hold one another up against gravity.

You are my sister, said the sister.

You are my reflection, said the sister.

You are the voice in my head.

And you are the face in my mirror.

They pulled and found themselves standing again, hands round waists, pressed close, the pubic hair growing together, binding them, hot, wet. The sister took her sister's neck in her hands, felt the heartbeat in her fingers, tickled the corner of her jaw, the joint of neck and skull, then pulled her close and kissed her long.

§

The sister watched the sister breathe in rasps, sweating. The sister took a cool damp towel to the sister's forehead. The sister rolled away, said she was cold. The sister climbed into bed beside her sister. Her face to the back of her head, her pelvis to her ass, her knees to hers, her feet to hers. The sister held her sister tight and fought against the nights that dragged her sister too soon from this life.

§

Time.

Dust drifted. Dust coated. Dust settled and wandered on. Dust grew and dust flew through the room they now lived in, the rest of the house falling to disuse. The dust covered the traces of their memories left in the scratches in wood, the burns in fabric, the stains in paint, the chips in glass. Dust did not consume but smeared the lens to the past and floated through the faint beams of light.

Time dragged the sisters at different rates, flung them forward and backwards, disrupting their constructed singularity.

And as they withered, the dust grew.

§

In the mornings the sister set the kettle for tea and readied breakfast for her sister.

Wake now, dear, the sister said touching her sister's shoulder.

It's you, said the sister. I dreamt of you.

The sister smiled, Come now, dear. Tea's ready.

I dreamt of you, her skeletal hands clawed towards her, gnarled by Time. I dreamt of you, she said again, the ravines deepening above her eyes, the lake of her mouth shrinking.

I know, dear. I dreamt of you, too.

I dreamt of you and now you're here. I dreamt there was another me. I dreamt of seeing me in another.

I know, dear. We always do. Gifted are we to have our dreams made true.

The sister shook her head, No.

She shook her head and stayed in bed.

The sister tried to feed her, to give her drink, but her sister would no longer speak, staring at her, distrustfully.

§

The sisters stood in line with the other girls, holding the bannister, watching the mirror. All dressed alike, in black leotards with white stockings, every girl's hair tied up in a bun, the sisters disappeared into the crowd of tiny girls. They ran round when class was done, playing with the other girls until the sister lost her sister. The sister cried and yelled for her sister but the sister did not hear. The sister pleaded for her sister to come but only Madame came and told her to stop this silliness but the sister stamped her feet and shook her fists, began pounding them against her own head and face until the tears were mixed with snot and blood and the sister returned, held her close, told her that they were sisters and would always be together as sisters, as one in two bodies.

§

I saw a star last night, the sister said to her sister.

Just one?

The sister nodded, There may be a million million stars but there is only this one star now, for me.

The sister watched her sister over breakfast, her hair cropped short and black, forehead smooth and white, eyes wide and out the window. The muscle in her neck and cheeks, the way her left eyelid twitched with her chewing, the sister memorised her sister's stare into the bluing sky where tangerine clouds splayed over the city.

What was it like?

The sister turned back to the sister, a smile parting her lips, You'll know it when you see it. I can see it even now in your eyes.

§

The sister slept fitfully while her sister wrote in her journal, the one she began to keep when her sister began to lose herself and the dust began to cover everything. She wrote and wrote, her hand cramping, gnarled by Time. The star shone beside the moon where it formed a triangle with Orion. The sister mapped constellations in her journal along with the degradation of her sister. She wrote one more line and closed the journal, returning to their bed, where she curled into her sister, a reflection of withered bodies wrapped fetally round an empty center.

CIPHER SISTERS

§

The sister woke before her sister. She opened her sister's journal and began to read. With every page finished, she ripped it from its spine and shoved it in her mouth.

What are you doing, said the sister.

The sister took the last page and shoved it in her mouth.

The sister rolled slowly from bed, sighing out more Time and dust, her bones creaking wilted gasps. The sister closed the journal and put on the kettle. A hand on her sister's shoulder, she said, I love you.

The sister stared back with her own eyes full of tears and wept without noise.

§

The father held the sisters in tattered photographs and the sisters looked at the sisters they once were. Children then, children still, yet crows now danced upon their eyes and skin fell heavier than it once did.

Remember how we used to be?

No, said the sister smiling.

Can you tell which one is which?

The sister laughed and kissed her sister.

I love you.

I am you.

We are more than two.

We are one.

The sister peeled away from the sister and opened the window, breathed in the summer air, the loose hairs floating in breeze.

The sister came behind her sister and held her, I love the mountains.

I know we do, she turned and threw her arms round her neck and kissed her until they tumbled back into their bed and fell into Time and the sister woke beside her sister and set the kettle and fixed breakfast while her sister slept. Wilted by time, the sister was slow and her back bent, Time weighing more and more with each passing dusted day.

Wake up, dear, the sister said to her sister, her voice weary, the dust thick and caught in her throat.

Wake up, dear, the sister pushed slightly against her sister's shoulder, dust clouding from contact.

Wake up, dear, her voice anxious. She put a hand to her sister's face and felt the cold breath of Time, the moist film of dust and old sweat.

Sister?

She stepped away, watching her sister no longer be a sister.

Sister, she fell backwards onto the ground, her back pressed against the wall, dust kicked into the air, a haze shrouding her sister from her.

Sister? She reached towards her sister as her eyes turned to dust.

Climbing into bed, the dust filled the room and she curled into her sister who was no longer a sister. She clung to the sister and wept, saying her name until there was no voice to say it and all was dust.

THUNDERDOME PRESS

ALSO AVAILABLE

In Search of a City: Los Angeles in 1,000 Words
(Available Now)

Los Angeles is whatever you want it to be, and nothing like you think. I gave these photos to a group of authors and asked them for precisely 1,000 words about what they saw. They didn't disappoint. Dreams, drugs, drama. Fame, famine, and fading glory. Few of the authors in this book have stepped foot in L.A., yet the soul of this city is so invasive and pervasive that the collection embodies everything that makes up this sprawling metropolitan mess. There's everyday life in Los Angeles, from the shiny dreams of the Hills to the hard realities of life in the Valley and out to the Inland Empire, and even more stories that are purely the stuff of dreams and fantasies, the kinds of worlds that exist only behind giant creaking doors on backlots scattered throughout the Southland. Whether you live here or just want to visit for a few moments, you're in for one hell of a ride.

Bloody Knuckles
(Fall 2013)

15 hard-hitting stories surrounding the world of Mixed Martial Arts. What does it mean to be a fighter? Why do we fight and why do people love to watch? This collection contains stories from notable crime fiction writers and true accounts from athletes who have spilled their own blood on the canvas, men and women who love the struggle of unarmed combat.

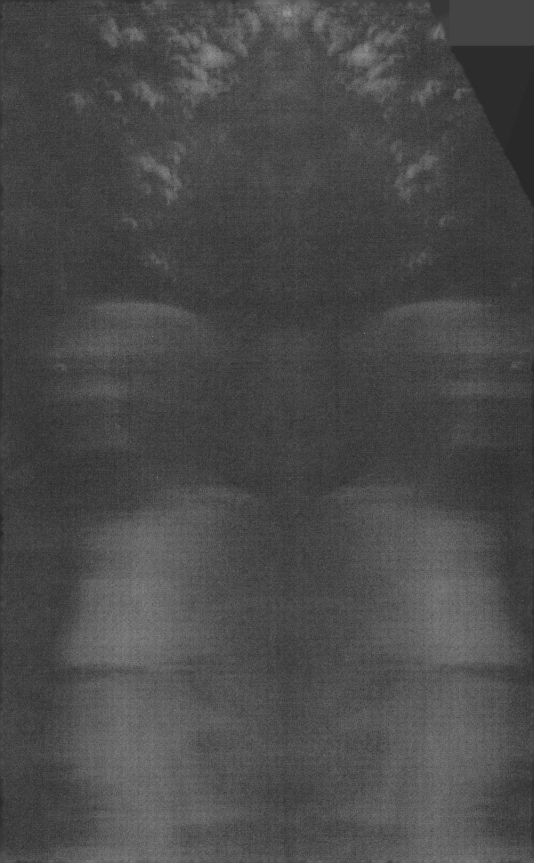

21182542R00068

Made in the USA
Charleston, SC
10 August 2013